WITHDRAWN

FLYING
CROWS

RANDOM HOUSE / NEW YORK

FLYING
CROWS

A NOVEL

Jim Lehrer

Copyright © 2004 by Jim Lehrer

All rights reserved under International and Pan-American Copyright
Conventions. Published in the United States by Random House,
an imprint of The Random House Publishing Group, a division
of Random House, Inc., New York, and simultaneously in Canada by
Random House of Canada Limited, Toronto.

RANDOM HOUSE and colophon are registered trademarks
of Random House, Inc.

Grateful acknowledgment is made to Brandt & Hochman Literary
Agents, Inc., for permission to reprint an excerpt from "John Brown's Body" from
John Brown's Body by Stephen Vincent Benét, copyright © 1927, 1928 by Stephen
Vincent Benét and copyright renewed © 1955, 1956 by Rosemary Carr Benét.
Reprinted by permission of Brandt & Hochman Literary Agents, Inc.

Library of Congress Cataloging-in-Publication Data
Lehrer, Jim.
Flying crows: a novel / Jim Lehrer
p.   cm.
ISBN 1-4000-6197-0
1. Psychiatric hospital patients—Fiction.   2. Homeless persons—Fiction.
3. Male friendship—Fiction   4. Missouri—Fiction.   5. Aged men—Fiction.
6. Boys—Fiction.   I. Title.
PS3562.E4419F58 2004   813'.54—dc22   2003058450

Printed in the United States of America on acid-free paper

Random House website address: www.atrandom.com

2 4 6 8 9 7 5 3 1

First Edition

Book design by Victoria Wong

TO OLIVIA — AND ANNETTE

Abide thou with me, fear not: for he that seeketh
my life, seeketh thy life: but with me
thou shalt be in safeguard.

—1 Samuel 22:23

KNIGHT I: Beware, My Lord, for the enemy's
spears come at us as straight as the crow flies.

KNIGHT II: Calm thyself, Sir, for not all
flying crows do harm.

—*Battle Royale,* Anon.

KANSAS CITY SOUTHERN
STRAIGHT AS THE CROW FLIES

I

RANDY

KANSAS CITY

1997

A private security firm had already done a search of the vast, mostly deserted Union Station building. But the contractor's insurance company, in consultation with the city manager's office, insisted that there be one final, thorough inspection supervised by the Kansas City Police Department. They wanted to make absolutely sure there was nothing on the premises—particularly no person or animal, dead or alive—that could, through legal action or other means, impede the important restoration work that was about to begin.

That was why Lieutenant Randy Benton and Luke Williams, a newly hired uniformed guard for the Union Station Rebirth Corporation, found a living person named Birdie.

That happened because of Randy's curiosity. He was a forty-five-year-old detective in the KCPD's Violent Crimes Division who had volunteered to be one of the twenty-five officers involved in the daylong sweep. Randy came from a Missouri Pacific family, his father having been a railroad policeman and his grandfather a brakeman in the yards at Winston, Missouri. As a kid, Randy's idea of heaven was to go to Union Station on Saturdays and Sundays to watch the trains and have a root beer float at the Harvey House soda fountain.

Here now was a wide full-length mirror hanging a few inches off the floor in what must have once been the Harvey House's storeroom or pantry. There was a dark wooden frame around the cracked and yellowed glass of the mirror. Even though scratched and dusty, he realized from its ornate, detailed etching of Roman soldiers on horses and elegantly dressed women in carriages that the piece was many years old, a special item—an antique—probably worth quite a lot.

Why would an expensive piece like this be hanging in a restaurant storeroom?

He tried to push the mirror to one side. It wouldn't move. He noticed two or three small hinges along the left side of the frame, so he grabbed the right side. The mirror swung easily away from the wall, like a door.

There behind the mirror was another door, also closed, slightly smaller than the mirror.

The real door, made of cracked and gray wood, had a white porcelain knob. Benton put an ear to the wooden panel. After a few seconds, he grabbed his pistol from its holster and motioned for Luke Williams to stand back. Williams was a former airport rent-a-car shuttle-bus driver in his late twenties, and this was his first law-enforcement episode. Instead of moving, he froze.

"I hear something," Randy whispered. He gave Williams another nod to move. This time, Williams did.

Randy shouted into the door, "Is anyone in there? This is the police! Kansas City PD!"

He waited and listened for a count of five. On ten, Randy turned the knob and pushed. The door opened easily.

"Please . . . don't hurt me . . . please. . . ."

It was the faint, weak, slow voice of a man.

Randy spotted somebody in the corner of a room that, without the light from his and Williams's flashlights, would have been pitch black. To Randy's hampered view, the place appeared to be no larger than a small closet, windowless and cluttered with stacks of books, newspapers, and other items hard to identify in the semidarkness. Randy also caught the smell of a burnt candle plus a faint whiff of cinnamon or nutmeg—some kind of spice.

There was a man sitting on the floor, his shaking hands held over the top of his head as if braced for a blow.

The detective stuck his pistol back in the holster. Then he and Williams, each grabbing an arm, lifted the feeble creature to his feet. He was as tall as Randy, almost six feet, but light as cotton. They guided him outside into the larger storeroom.

The man was elderly, well into his seventies, at least, Randy guessed. His face was partly obscured by wild growths of white hair and was bony and drawn, as was what could be seen of his fingers and arms. He was wearing a blue workshirt and a pair of black flannel pants that were wrinkled and filthy. The garments, to Randy, had an otherworldly look.

"What are you doing in here—in Union Station?" Randy asked, as they leaned the man against a wall.

"This . . . is . . . where . . . I . . . live." The man spoke precisely as if he were just learning to speak, though his voice was cracking.

"Nobody lives in a train station," Williams said.

"What's your name?" Randy asked.

"Birdie."

"Birdie what?"

"Birdie. . . . Just Birdie."

"What's your last name?" Williams asked.

"Birdie . . . just Birdie. . . . Carlucci . . . right, Carlucci. . . . Name's Birdie Carlucci."

"OK, Carlucci," said Williams. "Where you from?"

"I'm an . . . escaped . . . lunatic."

Randy gave Williams a wave. *I* will handle the rest of the questioning, said the signal. "What did you escape from, Mr. Carlucci?"

"The . . . Somerset . . . asylum."

"How did you get here?"

"I came . . . with Josh . . . on . . . The Flying . . . Crow." Birdie Carlucci began to slip down the side of the wall; he seemed not to have the strength to remain standing. Randy knew all about The Flying Crow. It was a streamlined passenger train of the Kansas City Southern that had gone out of business at least thirty years ago.

Randy and Williams helped the old man to sit down with his back leaning against the wall, his legs folded underneath him.

Randy crouched down to be at eye level. In twenty-one years as a cop, the detective had learned to read eyes. Birdie Carlucci's set of black ones spoke only of fear, not danger.

"Who's Josh?" Randy asked quietly.

"He's . . . my friend . . . from Centralia."

"My aunt's a librarian in Langley, not far from Centralia." Randy looked back toward the door to the smaller room. "Where's Josh now?"

"Josh . . . loves books. So do I . . . now. He . . . spent all his time . . . in the library . . . at Somerset. He's . . . cured."

"Cured of what?"

"Of . . . seeing something awful."

"When did you and Josh come here to Union Station, Mr. Carlucci?"

"Sixty-three . . . years . . . ago."

Randy exchanged a few more words with Birdie Carlucci on the slow walk up the stairs to the grand lobby, which was no longer grand at all. It was a sad, depressing mess. On the floor were puddles of water and clumps of plaster that had fallen from the once-beautiful ceiling. There was an ugly empty space where the ticket offices with their brass grilled windows had been. The paint on the walls was peeling, cracked, and dirty.

Randy badly wanted to believe the promise from city and restoration project leaders that they were going to bring this place back to life in all its former glory.

"Where are you from originally, Mr. Carlucci?" Randy asked, as he moved through the lobby alongside the shuffling, frail old man.

"Here . . . Kansas City . . . really." Birdie was still talking in fragments, but deliberately now.

"You didn't live in that little room down there for sixty-three years, did you?" Randy asked.

"No . . . no. At first . . . I moved around . . . staying different . . . places . . . each night or two."

"What kinds of different places?"

"The waiting room . . . baggage rooms . . . down at a train shed . . . offices, stores . . . all over. This is a big, big building."

"How did you live?"

"It was . . . a great life."

Two uniformed KCPD officers met them in front of what Randy knew had been the newsstand under the huge clock, which was still hanging there. The clock wasn't running and the shop was boarded up with plywood.

Randy and Williams, the private cop, walked with Carlucci and the two officers out to a police squad car parked in the driveway in front of the large east doors.

Birdie Carlucci suddenly stopped and looked around at the few cars parked outside beyond the driveway.

"I was here. I saw it . . . but don't ask me anything. I'm not . . . going to tell you . . . anything. I know you want to hear about . . . Pretty Boy . . . and Righetti. I won't talk."

Pretty Boy. Righetti. Randy Benton knew the names from history but most recently from *Put 'Em Up!,* a new book he had just read about the famous Union Station massacre. Kansas City's best-known crime writer, Jules Perkins, had retold the story of how four lawmen and a prisoner were shot and killed—right here in front of the train station—early one morning in 1933. Pretty Boy Floyd, a well-known bank robber from Oklahoma, and his drunken sidekick, Adam Righetti, were identified as being two of the gunmen and were caught a year later in Ohio. Floyd was shot and killed; Righetti was taken alive and brought back to Missouri, tried, and electrocuted for murder. But according to Perkins's book, it's unlikely that Floyd or Righetti had anything to do with what happened at Union Station. Perkins maintained it was mostly an invention by J. Edgar Hoover to get publicity and power for his federal law enforcement organization, soon to be renamed the FBI.

"Back then, did you tell anybody what you saw?" Randy asked Carlucci, playing along rather than asking seriously.

The old man closed his eyes and shook his head.

One of the two uniformed officers moved to stand by the opened back door of the squad car. Randy and the other officer grabbed each side of Birdie to ease him into the rear seat.

Randy had seen terror on many faces in the line of duty. From what he saw now in the eyes and demeanor of Birdie Carlucci, he knew this man was truly afraid.

"Don't want . . . to go . . . back. Not now," he said, trying in vain to raise his voice to a shout. His whole body was trembling, as it had been earlier when they found him in the storeroom closet.

"Back where?" Randy asked.

"To Somerset . . . the asylum."

"Somerset's been closed down for years, Mr. Carlucci. They don't even have places like that anymore. These officers will take you to our police station for processing, and then you'll be turned over to somebody in the social services division. You'll be fine."

"Will . . . you tell Josh . . . where I am?"

"Certainly, Mr. Carlucci. What's his last name? Josh what?"

"Don't . . . know. He saw . . . the Centralia massacre."

Randy had only a vague notion of what had happened at Centralia. Some Union soldiers had been pulled off a train by a band of Confederate guerrillas. They were ordered to strip and then killed.

Randy told the two KCPD officers to treat Birdie Carlucci gently during the ride and the processing.

"Make sure nobody hurts him," Randy said.

And in a few moments, Birdie Carlucci was gone.

Randy wasn't sure he believed the old man's tale of living in Union Station for sixty-three years, much less about having witnessed the Union Station massacre. None of it sounded plausible. But as he watched the blue-and-white squad car make the loop in front of the station and go on out to Pershing Road, he knew he had to find out. Curiosity was Randy's stock-in-trade, both his chief strength and his weakness. He had trouble letting go.

Within a few minutes, back inside Union Station to continue his search, his curiosity about the old man began to subside. Randy told himself that Birdie Carlucci was probably just another mentally disturbed homeless guy who had gone off his medicine. Whatever, the case would soon no longer be the business of the police anyhow.

Too bad, thought Randy. There was something intriguing about the old man.

And very likable.

II

JOSH AND BIRDIE

SOMERSET

1933

Josh had been rocking in the common room for nearly ninety minutes when they hustled somebody in who smelled like bad meat and sat him down in the chair on his left.

"Hey, Josh, here's a new one named Birdie," said Alonzo, a bushwhacker who smelled like Ivory, the soap that floats. "Teach him how to rock the loonies away."

Bushwhacker was what everyone here at the Missouri State Asylum for the Insane at Somerset called the attendants. Somebody had used the name several years ago as a kind of pejorative joke, but it caught on and was now part of the accepted language. Josh knew about the original bushwhackers, barbaric bands of Confederate guerrillas who preyed on Union soldiers and sympathizers during the Civil War. Their worst crime, of course, was committed in Centralia on a group of Union soldiers. He was an expert on that.

Josh said nothing but continued to move his rocker forward and back, as he did most every afternoon around this time. He didn't even think much of anything except how stupid it was to have everybody rocking like this every day. Nothing ever got rocked away.

"See you later, Birdie," said Alonzo. "Watch Josh and see how he rocks. Rock, rock, rock, Birdie. Rock, rock, rock."

Josh kept rocking, his eyes focused on the buzz haircut of Streamliner, the man in the chair directly in front of him.

Without looking, Josh knew Alonzo was gone but this new guy, Birdie, wasn't rocking. The chair on his left—it was only ten inches away—was not moving. Most of the others in the room were rocking. He could hear the low sounds—*bump . . . ta, bump . . . ta, bump . . . ta, bump . . . ta*—on the wooden floor. Forward, *bump . . .* and back, *ta.* How many people in how many rocking chairs were lined up in this big room of gray walls, doors, and ceilings? One day he counted as far as seventy-seven. Another day he stopped counting at eighty-two. The chairs, all dark pine exactly like his, and the people, all lunatics, were lined up in straight rows eight across like soldiers. Or schoolchildren. Or sticks.

Lawrence of Sedalia, four rows down and to the left, was one of a few who never rocked. Josh had never seen Lawrence's chair actually move. Lawrence always just sat there during rocking time, still as one of those statues of Civil War soldiers on a courthouse square. The only time Lawrence moved was when he took off his clothes, which, he said, drove him crazy. The bushwhackers used to make him put his clothes back on, but lately they'd begun to leave him mostly naked. Sometimes they got him to sweep the floors with one of their big brooms. Sweeping was the other routine thing to do around here. Josh never noticed that anything was swept away either.

Josh looked to his left, at the new loony. He's just a kid, he thought. Not even twenty. Sitting there rigid as a tree. Black hair. Bright white skin. Moist, greasy. Needs a shave. But good features in the face. Dressed in blue work clothes—the patients' uniform—but stinking like moldy green hamburger meat. They should have bathed him—hosed him down or thrown him in a hydrotherapy tub or something—before putting him in those clean clothes.

His eyes were wide open.

That's the way Josh's own eyes used to be before Dr. Will Mitchell helped him start his Centralia performances. Maybe this kid Birdie would perform something that could help him too. It was kind of working for Streamliner. Not Lawrence, not yet. Who knew if it ever would for him? Maybe he'd end up with the incurables, mostly old soldiers who saw something in the war that made them crazy.

"Ever sat in a rocking chair before?" Josh whispered to the new kid, Birdie.

Only whispered talk was allowed during rocking time. Josh waited several minutes for an answer that didn't come.

Then he said, "All you have to do is put your feet down on the floor in front of you and push back. Do it gently. Let the chair rock you forward, and then push your feet against the floor again. Do it over and over. Nothing to it. That's mostly what we do is rock—in the morning for two hours, in the afternoon for two hours, and after supper for an hour before we go to bed—so you'd better start doing it. Look over here and watch me. See how I put my feet on the floor and push back and then the chair rocks forward and I do it again? Try it. You can do it. If you don't rock you won't have much to do here, just sweep the floor or go to the library. They've got big heavy push brooms for sweeping and polishing the floors, and you can do that all day, but it's not as good as rocking. So rock; try it. You can only go to the library in the morning. Did Alonzo say your name was Birdie? Birdie from where? Where in Missouri you from? Birdie as in *tweet-tweet*?"

The kid turned his head toward Josh.

"*Tweet-tweet,*" he said, in a voice that was the opposite of a bird's—or at least any bird Josh had ever seen or heard. (Had the world created new kinds of birds since he came here?) The boy talked like a grown man speaking in a sewer. Maybe he had been in a sewer and that's what his smell was instead of rotten red meat turned green. The kid's face certainly didn't match a sewer. The wet white skin was all slick, free of the sickening big pimples that were on the faces of so many of the kids who came here. Josh asked a doctor once if pimples were a sign of lunacy, and the doctor only laughed. Except for Will Mitchell, who was now long gone, that's the way doctors here handled most of the questions they were asked.

"Kansas City," said Birdie. "I'm from Kansas City. You?"

"Mostly from Centralia. I'm from Centralia."

"Never heard of it."

That made Josh want to yell something really bad at this tweet-tweet Birdie. Like, How stupid can you be to live in Missouri and not know about Centralia? Haven't you read any history? The Civil War in Missouri? But he caught himself in time and just said, "OK, then, fine with me. But start rocking, Birdie of Kansas City. You'll go even crazier if you don't rock. It's the only medicine they've got around here to calm you down besides a baseball bat and a lot of hot and cold water. They're working on some things with electricity and insulin and pills, but it's going to be a while before they know if they really work. So, for your own good, rock, Birdie of Kansas City."

For your own good, rock. Josh had an odd thought about this kid's own good. Josh had seen nothing in the guy's black eyes or in the way he moved the muscles of his face or anything else to mark him as a lunatic. Most of the others had some mannerism, even if it was only a peculiar stare or a hesitant way of speaking, or they constantly sniffed their noses or stuck fingers or dirty socks in their ears. . . .

The kid turned his head back straight and rocked. *Bump . . . ta, bump . . . ta.* He did it again and again. "That's great," Josh said, adjusting his own his rocking to be in sync with Birdie's. Forward they went together; back they went together. *Bump . . . ta, bump . . . ta, bump . . . ta, bump . . . ta.* They rocked together like two soldiers in a close-order drill parade.

"You're a rocking natural," Josh said after a while.

"It's making me sleepy," said Birdie. His voice was too loud for rocking time.

"It's OK to sleep," Josh said, as pleasantly and soothingly as he could, looking back over at the new kid from Kansas City. "I know about sleep because I couldn't do much of it for a long time when I came here."

"Why not?" the kid asked. He stopped rocking.

"Every time I closed my eyes, I'd see something awful that I'd seen before, and I'd scream and rant. That's why I'm here."

"That's it? That's what you do to show you're crazy?"

"Not everybody's the same kind of crazy, of course."

Josh saw a smile come across the face of Birdie of Kansas City. Only a slight one and only for a second. "Me too," Birdie said finally, as he turned back and resumed rocking. "That's my problem too. You bet. That's it. I close my eyes and scream. That's me too."

Josh wondered about that, but he also hoped Alonzo or one of the other bushwhackers didn't hear Birdie. Talking wasn't allowed during rocking time. One of them might come over and club the kid with one of those padded bats called Louisville Sluggers—Somerset Sluggers around here. Josh had always loved baseball, particularly the semipro ball they played in the small towns of Missouri.

Josh watched as Birdie's eyelids began to close.

Then, in a flash, the kid from Kansas City threw his hands up toward the gray lead ceiling and screamed loud enough to be heard all the way there.

"No! Nooooo! Stop! Don't shoot no more! No! No! The blood! Look at the blood!"

So the kid really did have a problem. Certainly he did. Why else would he be here? They don't send sane people to places like this.

Josh considered trying to help the kid, but he knew it was no use—not right now.

In a count of less than ten, Slim, a skinny bushwhacker, was standing there in front of Birdie and his rocking chair. In his two hands he was holding his Somerset Slugger, a baseball bat with a piece of old quilt wrapped around the fat part and held in place by large rubber bands.

Slim was a bushwhacker with a mouth of brown and yellow teeth. He swung the bat hard, the padded part smacking against the left side of Birdie's head. The sound was simply the sound of a padded baseball bat hitting a man's head. Josh knew it well. There was nothing to compare it with because it was not like any other sound he had ever heard.

Birdie was quiet, knocked cold, his head drooping down on his chest.

Josh had never stopped rocking: *bump . . . ta, bump . . . ta, bump . . . ta, bump . . . ta, bump . . . ta, bump . . . ta.*

He wondered what kind of awful bloody horrors Birdie saw when he closed *his* eyes? He wondered when the last time was that Birdie went to sleep naturally, without the help of something like a Somerset Slugger.

Bump . . . ta, bump . . . ta.

 "About the word *somerset.* It means somersault. Isn't that peculiar, Birdie? Isn't that hard to figure? Why would anybody name a town in Missouri after what clowns, tumblers, and acrobats do at the circus?"

Birdie, now into only his second day at the lunatic asylum, stared at Josh as if he were seeing somebody who really was a lunatic.

They were sitting next to each other for lunch in the dining hall at a table with several other patients. The food, which they had gotten on their own from a cafeteria line, was a cheese sandwich on plain white bread, a glass of milk, a green apple, and a cup of black coffee. There were thirty long tables with bench seats—fifteen for men on one side, fifteen for women on the other. The dining hall was painted lime green and was the size of a small high school gymnasium.

Josh was following the orders from a bushwhacker named Jack to give Birdie, the new kid from Kansas City, the lay of the land here at Somerset. It was an assignment they had begun to give Josh more and more, and he relished doing it.

"The people in the town of Somerset, the sane people, call our asylum the Sunset because there's no way to look west from anyplace in town without seeing mostly Old Main up here on Confederate Hill. You know, don't you, that that's where we are now, in Old Main, the biggest building on the grounds, if not in the whole state of Missouri?"

Birdie shook his head, as if Josh were speaking a foreign language.

The guy's clearly had a bad night, thought Josh. There's no telling what they did to him to get him to go to sleep.

But Josh had figured Birdie must have paid some attention to where he was being brought yesterday. This four-story structure of red brick, turrets, and tiny windows was so huge, so dominating, that it was not only impossible to look past it to the setting sun from Somerset; it could most likely be seen from across the state line in Kansas.

Josh remembered being brought here, straitjacket style, in the back of a marshal's open wagon, in 1905. He was wrapped in a gray woolen blanket with a rope tied around his chest, stomach, and legs because they were afraid he might throw a fit or try to escape. It seemed to him that he had seen a massive red building on the horizon, getting larger and larger, for miles and miles, hours and hours.

Would they ever get there? Would it be awful when they did?

"So, here we are at the Sunset in Somerset," Josh said now to Birdie, as if he were announcing the arrival of a train—or a wagon.

The Sunset in Somerset. Josh sometimes wondered if there could be a second meaning to *sunset*. Up here on the hill at the asylum, things always seemed to be getting darker, with the inmates' suns never doing anything but setting.

Josh repeated none of this wondering to Birdie. The new kid's mouth was full of sandwich. To Josh's disgust, Birdie had covered the cheese between the bread with a coating of salt and pepper. Birdie nodded but clearly did not care about this building or what the people in town called it or anything else. He was just hungry—and tired.

"What did they do to you last night?" Lawrence of Sedalia, half-dressed as usual, asked Birdie, who no longer smelled like spoiled hamburger. His black hair was mussed, his eyes were bloodshot, but other than that he seemed almost normal to Josh. There was no trembling in his hands. His glances seemed engaged.

"They put me in a big tub of hot water for most of the night and then knocked me out with something. I only came to a little while ago," said

Birdie, pausing in his eating. "I woke up screaming in a little locked room all by myself. There was no window, only a slit through the door."

"Why do you scream?" Josh asked.

"I told you. It's because I have the same craziness thing you do. I see awful things—blood and stuff—when I close my eyes."

"Whose blood and stuff?"

"Cops and a crook."

"Where?"

"At the . . . well, someplace like a train station."

That didn't make sense to Josh. They had trains and passengers at train stations, not the blood and stuff Birdie was talking about. This kid may be a lunatic like the rest of us but maybe not, Josh thought. Maybe all he does is lie himself crazy. Could that be possible? It was times like this when he really missed Dr. Will Mitchell.

"They told me not to try to sleep or even close my eyes again unless there was an attendant with me," Birdie said.

Josh knew what that meant.

"Meantime, they brought me here for lunch and told me to do whatever you do and what you tell me to do," Birdie said to Josh. "They talk like you're almost one of them."

"That's because he does an act in the John Paul Flynn Auditorium every Christmas and Fourth of July and Halloween," Lawrence of Sedalia said. He was about forty, fat, friendly, bald, hazel-eyed. "I hate Josh's act. It makes me sick." Lawrence closed his eyes, dropped his knife and fork, and covered his ears with his hands.

Streamliner said to Lawrence, "Tickets, please. Everyone must have a ticket." Nobody paid any attention to Streamliner.

Richard of Harrisonville, a patient sitting next to Lawrence, whispered to Birdie, "We figure Lawrence is the craziest one of us. Wait till you see him at the auditorium when Josh does his act, new boy. You'll see."

Richard was a squat fellow in his late thirties with smooth olive skin and a head of full dark-brown hair that he parted down the middle. His eyes seemed crossed; at least Josh had never seen both of them focused on the same thing at the same time. There were a lot of people at Somerset whose eyes were crossed or otherwise screwed up. Josh figured it was a sure sign of some kind of lunacy.

Still whispering, Richard leaned even more across the table to talk to

Birdie, one eye focusing off to the right and the other to the left. Josh knew what he was going to do. Richard loved to tell new patients—all of whom he called "new boy," regardless of their age—the story of how the John Paul Flynn Auditorium got its name.

"Today is Sunday, visitors' day," Richard said to Birdie. "Did they tell you that, new boy?"

Birdie, still trying to eat his lunch, shook his head.

"Before long—from one o'clock sharp until two o'clock sharp—people from town and anywhere else in the world can come in to visit or just walk the grounds and stare."

"Maybe some of my people will come see me," Birdie said with a smile, the first Josh had seen on the kid's face. But it seemed a bit phony, like he really didn't expect anybody to come. "So will all the girls who love me."

Richard went on with his story.

"It was a visitors' Sunday in March 1921, not that long ago, right, Josh? You were already here, right, Josh? You know what happened, right, Josh?"

Josh told Richard he was correct on all three counts, and Richard went on.

"John Paul Flynn was one of the four Flynn Brothers of Excelsior Springs. They operated the Flynn Circus that toured around Missouri, Kansas, Oklahoma, and Texas. You ever go to a Flynn Circus, new boy?"

Birdie, the new boy, said he hadn't.

"Maybe they didn't come to big cities like Kansas City. That's where you're from, right, new boy? You a crook like Pendergast and those Italians? You a whiskey runner or a gambler, like most everybody I ever heard of from Kansas City on the Missouri side?"

Josh watched Birdie for some reaction, but the kid's face showed nothing beyond the fact that he was listening and not caring much about what he was hearing.

Richard didn't wait for an answer anyhow. He just went on, still in a whisper.

"John Paul came here to Somerset that Sunday afternoon to visit one of his brothers, Ronald James Flynn. He was thirty-two years old; John Paul was thirty-seven. Ronald had been committed here because every private hospital and doctor his rich family found couldn't cure him of his particular kind of lunacy. And, oh, boy, did he have a particular kind. Ronald, poor soul, had worked with the family circus's lions and tigers and, after a while, began to take on the sounds and movements of a ferocious lion. Right, Josh? You were here, Josh. Tell him I'm right."

"Being a lion," Josh said, "was, in fact, Ronald's sickness."

Richard picked up his story. "On that Sunday, an ordinary one just like today, Ronald was allowed to walk around the grounds and Old Main with his brother without a bushwhacker or a Somerset Sister or anyone else watching over him. That was a mistake, wasn't it, Josh?"

Josh nodded. Birdie had quit eating altogether. He was listening intently.

"Because while strolling about, seemingly peaceful and all," Richard said, "Ronald coaxed his brother John Paul into the empty auditorium—at that time named for no one—to watch a new act he said he had created for their circus. You can guess what happened, can't you, new boy?"

Birdie just sat there calmly looking at Richard, ready to hear the end of the story.

"Well?" said Richard. "What's your guess, new boy? What do you think happened?"

"Don't make him guess," Lawrence whined. "Just tell him."

"All aboard for The Flying Crow to Hummer and Kansas City," Streamliner said. "Have your tickets ready. The sleeping car is the last one right before the club observation car. . . ."

Richard was determined to tell the story his way, which was always to drag it out as long as possible. There were rituals to most everything in life here at the Sunset in Somerset, just like there were at church and at lodge meetings and most everywhere else in the outside world. Josh knew there was no way Richard would change the speed of his storytelling—the ritual—for anybody, most particularly a new boy.

Richard bit into his apple, chewed the mouthful five, six, seven times. Then he took another bite and did it all again. He had two sips of coffee, after first blowing on it to make it cooler, an act that was strictly for show. That coffee had come out of the big stainless-steel pitcher already lukewarm.

Then he started whispering again.

"A bushwhacker, alerted by the sound of frantic screams for help, ran in too late to save John Paul from being mangled to death, lion style, by Ronald. Ronald killed his brother like a lion would kill a sheep or a deer or a big-game hunter. It happened right in the center of the stage where Josh does his Centralia act."

Birdie continued not to eat, only to look at Richard as if he was—well, crazy.

"The asylum superintendent quickly decided to name the auditorium in memory of the dead brother and to lock up the other brother in Beech. He hasn't been seen since, has he, Josh?"

Josh agreed; to his knowledge, Ronald Flynn had never been seen outside the asylum's Beechcraft Wing.

There were three wings of patient rooms and dormitories that went out like appendages from Old Main. They had been named for airplane manufacturing companies by an asylum superintendent who, the story went, had grown up in Wichita, Kansas, where inventing, making, and flying small airplanes was a common enterprise. So there was the Stearman Wing, where Josh and the rest of the men lived, and the Cessna Wing for women on the other side. There was almost complete segregation between the men and women, the only time they ever saw one another being across their separate eating sections in the dining hall and out on the grounds doing their respective organized activities.

The third wing, which ran out the back of Old Main, was the Beechcraft Wing, called simply Beech, which was where the hopeless were housed: the incurable, the demented, the very old, and those physically ill with TB or something else besides insanity who were kept away from the rest of the asylum society to die out of sight. There was a large locked double door leading off to Beech. Josh had never been on the other side of it, and he had never talked to anyone who had.

Richard, his story finished, stood up and left the dining hall without a word or smile. That was what he always did, Josh explained to Birdie.

"Is that true, what he said?" Birdie asked.

"I'm afraid so," Josh said.

"How could a man become a lion?"

"Wait till you hear Josh's Centralia story," Lawrence said. "It's much, much worse."

Lawrence also rose and departed. So did Streamliner and most of the others around them.

It was almost one o'clock, according to the large clock on the far wall over the door that led out to the hallway toward Stearman. Time for visiting hour to begin.

The bushwhacker named Jack came for Birdie. "Josh and I will take you to your space in the dormitory—your new home away from home, bud," he said, in his foreign accent. When Josh first heard him he thought it was British, but, as it turned out, Jack was from New Zealand. He had come to Missouri with a nurse from Somerset he had met and married some other place far away—someplace like Malaysia, Singapore, China, Korea, or Australia. Now they both worked at the Sunset.

"Don't worry about any visitors who might come for you, bud," said Jack. "I'll get you if they do."

Jack was a tall well-built bushwhacker who never used a cussword or a Somerset Slugger on patients. He had been known to use his fists, which were large and soft, on a chin or a head, but usually gently and mostly only to put somebody to sleep—or out of his misery. He also used a soft rope instead of the regular hard leather straps as restraints.

Birdie dismissed Jack's comments about visitors with no sign of concern. That told Josh the kid from Kansas City was definitely only blowing smoke when he talked about his people and girls coming.

Josh and Birdie fell in together, Jack following them as they left the dining hall.

"How did you get the name Birdie?" Josh asked.

"My Aunt Grace, who was beautiful, gave it to me when I didn't eat all my food one day," said Birdie. "She said I'd get as skinny as a bird on a skinny tree limb if I didn't eat more. '*Tweet, tweet, tweet,* little birdie.' And I was Birdie."

"What was your name before it was Birdie?"

"What are you doing, taking the census for the government? My Aunt Grace's husband—her second or third, I think—worked for the post office at Christmastime. The rest of the year he didn't do much of anything the best I could tell, but nobody else was doing much either until Roosevelt came in because of Tom Pendergast."

Because of Tom Pendergast? They didn't let patients read the daily newspapers, but Josh had heard some of the bushwhackers talk about the Pendergast machine in Kansas City. What he knew was that the machine was crooked and rough and tough but he didn't know they were responsible for Roosevelt—the one who was president now. Josh had heard about Teddy Roosevelt, who was a Rough Rider in glasses with no rims, but he knew little or nothing about this second one they called by his initials, FDR. He had the impression from God knows where that Roosevelt Two was the fault of a president named Herbert Hoover, who didn't think there was anything wrong with people standing in breadlines. That's what a bushwhacker named Jefferson said one time while he was running water in the tub for a hydrotherapy treatment. Josh couldn't remember exactly how long ago that was or how it had come up in the conversation. Jefferson normally didn't talk much about anything. *Jefferson.* Now there was a good name to have.

Birdie didn't respond to Josh's census question. It didn't really matter. Josh was only asking questions out of simple old-fashioned curiosity. He himself was Joshua Alan Lancaster, but the name no longer had meaning. He hadn't been called anything but Josh since he came to Somerset. Nobody except doctors and the superintendent, not even the bushwhackers, used last names. Birdie was Birdie, and as long as he was at Somerset that was all he would be.

The no-last-name thing was even true of the volunteers from town, including the Somerset Sisters. That came to Josh's mind right now because here came his favorite, Sister Hilda, down the hallway.

"Josh, Josh, good morning," she said with a wide smile.

"Good morning to you, Sister Hilda," said Josh.

Without having to look, Josh could feel the heat of excitement gushing out of the kid Birdie. It was certainly understandable. Mrs. Hilda Owens, the young wife of the vice president of the Somerset Bank & Trust Company, was a strikingly beautiful woman who, particularly from the side, seemed all set for a shampoo advertisement in a magazine. Her hair was bright yellow, her skin milky white, her lips large and red. The shape of her body, clearly discernible through a red-and-white flowered dress, would, as they say, turn a pope's head.

"This is Birdie," Josh said. "He just came in yesterday."

"Well, Birdie, welcome to Somerset," said Sister Hilda in a voice that was light, airy, musical. "I hope you are a poetry fan like Josh."

"I am, I am. I love poetry. Yes, ma'am. I love every word of it." Birdie's words jumped out of his mouth like popping corn.

"That's wonderful. Be sure and come to my reading on Tuesday. I'm planning to read some of Vachel Lindsay and Henry Wadsworth Longfellow."

"I'll be there. I will, I will, I will."

As she walked on, Birdie watched her every moving part, most particularly her magnificently rounded rear end and her legs, visible through straight-seamed silk stockings, which were perfectly formed.

"On with ya, bud," Jack the bushwhacker said.

Birdie seemed unable to move. "Who is she? Why is she here?"

"She's what they call a Somerset Sister," Josh explained. "That's the same as gray ladies in hospitals. They come here to help during Sunday visiting hour and do other things for the patients."

"What kind of other things?" Birdie asked, with a silly grin on his face.

"Let's get a move on, buddies," said Jack.

"I could tell just now that she liked me," Birdie said to Josh, once they started walking again. "Didn't you see the way she smiled at me? Women all do that."

Josh was struck by how rare it was for a Somerset patient to say anything routinely normal about a reaction to a woman.

But as they arrived at a large locked door that led to Stearman Wing, Josh thought it best to issue a warning. He said to Birdie, "There once was a patient, a handsome fast-talker from Webb City, who thought he saw the same thing in a Somerset Sister who was the wife of a lawyer in town. He tried to act on it, she told everybody, and they beat his head so hard and so often with sluggers that within a week he was dead from what they called *brain poisoning*."

Josh didn't think Birdie heard what he said because the new boy from Kansas City still had that silly—normal—smile on his face.

The curtain opened for Josh. There he stood, dressed in short dark-green pants and a white shirt with bloused sleeves and a large collar. His flowing hair looked very appropriate with that outfit. He was greeted by a loud noise of clapping and shouting.

John Paul Flynn Auditorium had the appearance and feel of a second-rate theater or opera house. Its main floor slanted up from a three-foot-high stage. There were several dressing rooms in the back and a curtain of heavy red velvet across the front. There were some four hundred folding wooden chairs arranged in a half-moon on the slanted floor and another hundred seats in a one-tier balcony. Christmas and other holiday pageants and performances by asylum musical and dramatic groups were held here.

Josh bowed with a flourish and then stood up like a soldier snapping to attention. Looking straight ahead toward the back of the hall, making no eye contact with anyone, he spoke in a stiff, formal manner, very different from his usual way.

"This account I am about to give to you comes from my own experience as a participant and eyewitness to one of the most barbaric massacres in the history of our state of Missouri, if not our world. The story I will now tell is as weird a tale as ever grew out of the most vivid imagination of any writer of fiction."

Josh paused and moved his eyes around the auditorium. It was a crucial part of his opening ritual. Hear ye, hear ye, listen up! That was the message, the order of the day.

Everyone obeyed. Some four hundred people, patients and staff, sitting in chairs and standing around on the sides, were quiet.

"If anyone here is a person prone to fits of fear or screaming when confronted with tales of savagery, gore, and horror, I would advise them now either to leave the room, which they can't do without permission, or close their eyes and ears, which they can do on their own. Because I hereby forewarn everyone present that what you are about to experience, through the straightforward, unembellished, true, and accurate recitation of my experience as a small boy in Centralia, is something that can only bring you to the outer limits of your ability to tolerate savagery, gore, and horror."

The words and sentences came out like they were part of sharp turns at the corners of a box. If the people in the audience hadn't known for sure already who he was, they might well have thought Josh, this man onstage dressed like a kid, was really somebody else.

"Like the radio show or a burlesque moving picture, only everybody dies!" one of the patients yelled, as was usual at this point in the program.

Josh did not respond. He acted, as always, as if he had not heard.

Then he slowly, deliberately, turned his back on the audience, which momentarily created absolute silence. The new patients who were seeing this for the first time were shushed silent by fellow patients and bushwhackers.

That was because Josh's about-face signaled that his Massacre Act was about to begin. Silence, everyone!

"Let me out of here! Please! Let me out!"

That was Lawrence of Sedalia in the front row, where the bushwhackers always made him sit. Lawrence was simultaneously trying to hold his hands over his eyes, his mouth, and his ears while screaming and crying and sobbing. He pleaded with the bushwhackers not to make him see Josh's show again, but they always insisted that he do so. It's good therapy for you,

Lawrence, they said. Witnessing Josh getting over his problem will give you the strength and hope to get over your problem someday.

Nobody seemed to know exactly what Lawrence's problem was, but they mostly called it civilian shell shock. Lawrence walked around the asylum almost always naked because clothes reminded him of something awful he had witnessed in Sedalia, a town in central Missouri. Supposedly, what he saw was his uncle, a Holiness preacher from Texas, tear the clothes off his wife and two infant children and then drown them in a lake to protect them from the spirit of the devil that was moving toward Sedalia from Durant, Oklahoma. To Josh, Lawrence mostly seemed shy and withdrawn and off in another world, except when he was watching Josh's Massacre Act. Would being scared cause him to put his clothes on, rid him of his shyness, and chase out his demons?

Josh was sure the bushwhackers permitted his regular performances because it gave them pleasure to watch him terrify Lawrence and the other lunatics, but he hated to think about that. He wasn't onstage tonight or any other night to understand or feel guilty; he was there to be the star, to entertain, to be a swell example, to be the patient who had made the greatest progress in overcoming his lunacy by standing up in front of a group of fellow lunatics and scaring them out of their wits.

III

RANDY

KANSAS CITY

1997

Randy was working an overnight armed robbery at an apartment near the Country Club Plaza. A uniformed patrol squad had brought in a thug to city jail this morning they thought might be good for it.

The man in custody was somebody Randy had encountered more than once. He was not only willing to talk about last night's robbery but would also implicate others in exchange for a break on a possible habitual-criminal charge. Randy said he would pass that on to the district attorney's office. And that was that.

On his way out of the small jail conference room, Randy passed by the Cage, one of the holding cells where as many as twenty or twenty-five prisoners were kept temporarily while their cases were processed. It was a crowded, noisy, awful place to be—and sometimes even dangerous for prisoners not used to this rough, violent, profane world.

Randy, his mind on the robbery suspect, hadn't even glanced in the cell on his way to the interview, but now he did. And there, huddled in one corner, his head down and his hands around his legs, was an old man with wild white hair.

It was the Union Station bum! The guy they'd found yesterday. What was his name? Birdie. Right. Birdie . . . something.

Randy was furious. He began to count to ten—maybe even thirty or forty for this one. He had a hot temper that he worked hard at controlling, in the interests of advancing his police career as well as his family life. His promotion to sergeant a few years back had been delayed three months while he underwent counseling by a psychologist who specialized in anger management. That grew out of his throwing a heavy metal chair from a window of the detectives' squad room when informed of a judge's decision to put a particularly vicious holdup man back on the street. The chair fell four floors to the street, barely missing the head of a passing pedestrian.

Counting before acting on a particular burst of rage was the cure.

He was up to thirty-five by the time he arrived at the main processing desk to confront the sergeant in charge about Birdie . . . Carlucci? Yes. Birdie Carlucci was what he had said his name was.

"I just saw a guy named Carlucci in the Cage," Randy said. His upper lip was quivering, but otherwise he was in control. "He's a sick old man who needs help from social services. What's going on?"

The sergeant, younger but as rough and ready as Randy, looked at some papers. "The computer maybe came up with a *wanted* on him, I don't know. Maybe we're waiting for some clarification. He'll most probably be out of here to a group house somewhere."

"He escaped from a state hospital more than sixty years ago! At least put him in a cell by himself. He'll get eaten up in the Cage."

The sergeant agreed, and in a few minutes Randy went with a jail guard to the Cage to retrieve Carlucci and settle him into an individual cell. It was small but it was clean and had a cot, a chair, and its own commode.

"Did you find Josh . . . yet?" Carlucci asked Randy, once the guard was gone. Without being invited, Randy sat down in the chair and motioned for Carlucci to sit on the cot. The old man's speaking, while still deliberate, was not as halting as it had been. But he did seem sick—and more frail even than when they found him two days ago.

"No, I haven't had a chance to get on that yet," Randy said. "To tell you the truth, without his last name I don't even know where to begin."

"Centralia. I said he was . . . from Centralia. They would . . . know where he is. He was from Centralia."

Randy said he would try Centralia. "I'm sorry you got tossed in that holding cell, Mr. Carlucci. We call it the Cage and that's about all it is. Are you feeling all right?"

"I'm fine, thank you. I . . . didn't mind that many people. It has . . . been a long time."

"I assume they've given you plenty to eat? You still look pretty weak."

"I am not really . . . hungry."

"How did you eat while you lived at Union Station?"

"At first, mostly with help from a wonderful Harvey Girl . . . Janice. She gave me leftovers. I ate like a king. When the Harvey House closed, it was . . . much harder. And it was really hard after the last restaurant closed, the one that came in after the Harvey House."

In Randy's mind, the Union Station had begun its real decline when the Harvey House closed in the 1960s. Randy was fourteen or fifteen at the time. He had read a story in the *Star* that said Kansas City hadn't been the same since, and he was inclined to agree. Even though he had had little more than sweets and sandwiches there, he considered every bite or sip of what he consumed at the Harvey House to have been memorable.

"Janice?" Randy asked, almost by reflex. "Did she have a last name?"

"I am sure she did . . . but she never told me what it was. We had some great times together . . . and not just eating."

"Where, exactly?"

"At Union Station."

Randy was as confused as he was curious. But he had to get on to the district attorney's office.

He left Birdie Carlucci with the assurance that it wouldn't be long before a social worker helped find him someplace to go besides a jail cell. Most likely, in a community-based group housing facility run by the city-county health services people.

"We don't put folks like you in jail anymore, Mr. Carlucci," he said at the cell door, "and, like I told you before, all the state hospitals—you know, for people with your kind of problems—are closed."

"I'm not a lunatic. I mean . . . not anymore."

Randy thought of Carlucci's desire for Randy to contact Josh.

"When was the last time you saw your friend Josh?"

"Oh, that was the day I came . . . to Union Station: in 1933."

"How old was he at the time, do you remember?"

"He was pretty old, sixty or seventy . . . something like that."

"How old are you, by the way?" Randy asked. This would definitely be his last question.

"About the same as Josh . . . was."

Randy promised to stay in touch.

And suddenly his curiosity about this man had returned—big time.

Janice the Harvey Girl. As a kid, Randy had had many a wet dream while imagining what treasures and pleasures lay in wanton waiting under all those layers of Harvey Girl skirts and aprons and stockings.

IV

JOSH AND BIRDIE

SOMERSET

1933

Josh heard the duty doctor tell the bushwhackers that there was something *insincere* about Birdie. "I'm not sure he's a maximum lunatic," said the doctor. But he told them to be prepared for Birdie to make some noise and commotion and possibly even do something violent. The doctor, as always, then left the asylum and its patients to the care of the bushwhackers. He would do the rest of his Sunday night on-call duty from his home in town.

The doctor was a young man named Jameson who, from Josh's observation, was not competent to trim a toenail, much less deal with lunacy—sincere or otherwise. Josh had come across only one fine doctor in all his years at Somerset. He was Dr. Will Mitchell, a good man, a helpful, caring soul, who tried as best as he could to guide Somerset patients back to sanity and a regular life. Dr. Mitchell had been extremely helpful to Josh. He had, in fact, saved Josh's life—and soul. Dr. Mitchell had left Somerset in anger thirteen years ago to become a private doctor in Kansas City.

Among the practices at Somerset that enraged Dr. Mitchell was the use of Somerset Sluggers. Nor did he like the kind of restraining they were doing to Birdie this night.

Just before lights-out at nine, the bushwhackers held Birdie down on his back while they tied his hands and arms to the metal frame of his bed. It was a common practice. Five other patients considered to be violent or potential wanderers were routinely strapped down on this ward.

"That way, no matter what, and just in case he decides to play games," said Amos the ass, the night bushwhacker in charge, "this Birdie can't fly away and damage anybody, including his ownself, can he?"

Amos said that to Josh, whose bed was directly across from Birdie's. The long narrow dormitory room had two rows of twenty single beds each, lined up barracks-style on both sides of a center aisle with the heads of the beds against a wall. All but two of the forty beds were occupied now, Birdie having just become the thirty-eighth patient on the ward.

"Help us keep an eye on your young friend over there," said Amos, knowing Josh would do that without having to be asked. From head to head, counting the twelve-foot aisle, Josh was barely twenty-five feet away from Birdie.

Josh didn't really know what to make of what the doctor and the bushwhackers were saying about Birdie. He had heard rumors that sometimes sane people were sent here for personal, family, or political reasons, but he had never come across one. Josh did think the new boy, this Birdie from Kansas City, seemed pretty normal until he saw what happened when the kid closed his eyes during that first rocking time. Only lunatics screamed when they closed their eyes.

Josh kept his own eyes wide open now while he braced for the worst from Birdie. But after a few minutes of silence from across the way, Josh's own lids began to droop and he launched the nightly ritual that he and Dr. Mitchell had invented years ago. Moving his lips but with no sound, Josh said, "I have to say now, dear listener, as I approach a description of the final horrors of the massacre, my voice grows weak, my sight is dimmed, and my heart sickens with the recollection. . . ."

Now his eyes were closed, and the threat of his own screaming eruption had passed. He moved his mind to thinking about his annoyance about where they had put Birdie. He was in a bed that, for Josh, was still warm with the body heat and juices as well as the soul of Jesus of Chillicothe, who had died in his sleep just nine days ago. There were two other vacant beds down at the other end of the room. Too bad they couldn't put Birdie in one of them. But that would have made it impossible for Josh to keep watch on him.

Josh thought about Jesus of Chillicothe. They never said why he died. He just didn't wake up one morning, after complaining for two days about feeling as if a wagon of dirt were being pulled back and forth over his chest by twelve horses and experiencing wild tingling in both of his arms. Josh was one of four patients who were allowed to attend a brief burial service down at the Unknowns Cemetery under the trees alongside the Kansas City Southern tracks. The Methodist minister from town who presided spoke only of "the deceased"; he never mentioned a name, either a real one or Jesus of Chillicothe, as the dead man had called himself for the twenty-four years he had been a Somerset patient. Josh once asked Jesus, a gaunt figure in his late fifties when he died, where he was from and why he was sent to Somerset. Jesus said he was working for the Livingston County agricultural agent in Chillicothe, counting the number of acres growing wheat, when God ordered him, his son Jesus of Chillicothe, to quit counting the acres and set them all on fire. "Unfortunately, God the Father chose to take the lives of two farm families along with the wheat," he said. That led to Jesus of Chillicothe being ajudged a lunatic and committed here in lieu of being hanged for murder. The headstone they put over the grave had only a number on it: *371*. The administration office usually didn't pay attention to names after a patient had been in the asylum for twenty years or more without a visitor or an inquiry. Jesus of Chillicothe, who could recite most every word of the New Testament from memory, never had either. Neither had Josh.

For the first half hour now, the only noise in the ward came from the usual farts, belches, giggles, and whispered conversations and the continual barely audible orders from Streamliner for everyone to have their tickets ready before he went off into his go-to-sleep ritual of reciting the opening lines of Josh's Centralia massacre story. Then, like the beginning rolls of a coming storm, the other noises, including Streamliner's, ended and the snoring began as, one by one, the men fell asleep.

Josh wanted to read, to move his mind far away from this place and even the question of Birdie's bed and the death of Jesus of Chillicothe. He had the asylum library's copy of Stephen Vincent Benét's *John Brown's Body* in the top drawer of his bedside table, one of the two-foot-square white metal cabinets put between the beds for each patient. If anybody had more stuff than would fit in the cabinet, it went under the bed. Josh had nothing under his bed; as far he knew, neither did anybody else. Patients came to Somerset with nothing but a few clothes and toilet articles, and it stayed that way because there was no way—or need—to acquire anything else.

But it was impossible for Josh to read in this darkness. There had been a time when he could see the print of a book pretty well at night, having been taught by a bushwhacker war veteran how to train his eyes for night vision. But it was getting increasingly difficult for Josh to read even in the broadest daylight. Sister Hilda, his favorite Somerset Sister, had brought him a large magnifying glass and had promised to get the local optician to make him a pair of reading glasses someday. . . .

Josh heard a metallic rattling sound, one of the tied-down patients jerking on his ropes. It had to be Birdie. The others seldom did it anymore; they knew it was useless. They had learned that if they had a real emergency, or even if they just had to go to the bathroom, the only way they could get loose was to yell out loudly and long enough to bring a bushwhacker into the ward. Pulling on the ropes got you nowhere.

The rattle stopped. Birdie must have also figured out those ropes weren't going to break or come loose. Would he close his eyes and try to go to sleep? Josh held his breath. The only sound was that of snoring, some occasional dialogue from a dream, the scream from a nightmare. Somebody—it sounded like Gardner from Lee's Summit, ten beds away from Josh—was being chased by a white mouse. Another guy was denying to a woman, probably his wife, that he had touched her baby sister while she slept on a sunporch. Somebody else, Josh couldn't tell for sure who, was reciting a recipe for corn-bread stuffing over and over.

Then it began.

"No! No! Don't shoot no more! The blood! Look at the blood!" Birdie's voice was a piercing screech. "Nooooooooooooo!"

Josh sat up in bed.

"Don't shoot no more! The blood! Nooooooo!"

One of the other patients yelled halfheartedly, "Knock it off, new boy. Us lunatics need our beauty sleep too." Josh, even in the dark, knew that was Richard of Harrisonville.

"The blood! Don't shoot no more!"

Figuring it wouldn't be long before a bushwhacker would be in here, Josh decided to do something. The bushwhackers, as Amos had done tonight, encouraged him to act in situations like this. He slipped his blue cotton pants over his underwear, stuck on his shoes, and went over to Birdie's bed.

"Hey, Birdie, it's me, Josh," he whispered. He leaned down into Birdie's face, which was twisted like a dirty rag. "Forget about what happened to you. Tell me a story of something else, Birdie. Tell me a story, any story. . . ."

At that moment, the lights came on, the hallway door sprang open, and in rushed Amos and two other bushwhackers carrying Somerset Sluggers.

They untied Birdie and yanked him to the floor. Then they ordered him to strip naked and led him away. As they left the ward, they invited Josh to join them.

The bushwhackers didn't slug Birdie in the head because he went quietly. He was through screaming. Josh figured that was because he was wide awake and his eyes were no longer closed.

"Please let me put some clothes on," Birdie said to the bushwhackers. He said it quietly, like a normal person would.

"Forget it," Amos said, and he pushed Birdie on in front of him.

Josh saw how truly upset Birdie was about being naked in front of him and the bushwhackers—all men. He was walking pigeon-toed, with his hands covering his genitals. That reaction, in his pre-Somerset life many years ago, would have seemed completely normal to Josh. But forcing patients to be naked was an accepted way of life here at Somerset. It was another of those routine tools of control and discipline that so upset Dr. Will Mitchell.

They took Birdie to the hydrotherapy room, which was a steamy, soapy, all-white room with a tile floor that was only big enough for two large bathtubs and an open stall of four shower nozzles. As Josh saw it, hydrotherapy was a fancy word for a long bath or shower. Sometimes the water was hot, sometimes cold. Sometimes it calmed down agitated or energized patients, sometimes it didn't. Mostly, it seemed to Josh, it just made them wet.

Within minutes, Birdie was lying in a tub of hot water. Birdie didn't seem to mind. He was still holding his privates underwater but his face was not twisted and contorted as it had been when he was screaming.

"Talk to him, Josh, do your thing on this guy—if you can," said Amos, ignoring the fact that Birdie was as quiet as a mouse now. "I've got to check on some guy who's crapped in his bed over in Five Ward."

Josh would indeed try his thing on Birdie. To be helpful, to work with new patients, was part of the deal he had made with Dr. Mitchell, who said—and convinced the superintendents and the bushwhackers—it might be good treatment for Josh as well as the other patients. Josh took seriously his mission to try to provide help to some of his fellow lunatics. He could not claim any cures, but that didn't seem to matter because that was not what this asylum was in business to do. Will Mitchell was probably right when he had said over and over that care and feeding was really the main purpose of the Sunset at Somerset. But Josh had had some triumphs, his most notable being Streamliner. And it was the story of Streamliner that Josh always used on newly arrived patients.

Josh pulled a wooden stool up to the side of Birdie's bathtub.

"You know the man we all call Streamliner, Birdie? I have no idea what his real name is. Bob? Bill? Jack? Matthew, Mark, Luke, or John—who knows? He's Streamliner."

Birdie moved one hand off his genitals. That was a good sign. He was relaxing, he was listening.

"I want to tell you about him, Birdie. Maybe you could learn from what happened to him. I think it could be an inspiration to you. OK?"

Birdie, not looking at Josh, made no response. But Josh didn't mind. He kept talking.

"Well, you can sure tell that name doesn't have anything to do with his appearance, right? He's lumpy and plumpy and cuts his hair short. He's twenty-two years old. Would you have guessed that? I didn't. He seems much older, doesn't he? He sure does. That's because of what happened to him. It not only touched him in his mind, like your and my experiences did—"

"That's right." Birdie interrupted Josh. "We had experiences that made us nuts. We can't sleep. That's what's wrong with you, and that's what's wrong with me. That's my disease. That's why . . . yeah, that's why they sent me here. Yeah, that's it. That's why I'm here. If anybody asks you, you tell 'em I'm really nuts. You tell 'em, OK? Why else would I put up with getting whacked and drowned? You tell 'em, Josh."

Josh nodded, as if understanding and sympathizing, agreeing to tell everybody Birdie was a lunatic.

Then he went back to talking about Streamliner. "I was just saying that, as you could see, he looks nothing like a streamliner train, not that I have seen one of those except in magazines myself."

Birdie smiled. "I've seen 'em many times, up close. I love the streamliners. They're magic. The Santa Fe has the best, going to California and Chicago. You can see the fancy people inside, eating off tablecloths, reading the newspaper. Someday they're going to make the streamliners all silver and run them on something besides steam. That's what they're talking about, at least."

Josh was delighted by Birdie's excitement. "You should talk to Stream-liner about trains."

Birdie shook his head at that suggestion.

"Well, have you heard of a train called The Flying Crow?" Josh asked.

"Yeah, yeah. It's the Kansas City Southern's streamliner from Kansas City to Texas; it comes right by here, I think. 'Straight as the Crow Flies.' That's the company's motto."

Josh said, "Right, the tracks are at the bottom of the hill between here and town. The point is, Streamliner's nickname came from his believing he's a conductor on The Flying Crow. You heard him."

"Yeah, but I didn't know exactly what he was doing. I just figured he was crazy."

"That's right, he is. But he's doing better."

Birdie turned away and settled deeper into the water, which was now just under his chin. He seemed to have lost interest in Streamliner's story.

But Josh went on anyhow.

"Streamliner's problem was caused by having witnessed something awful. He and his sister were walking to their one-room school on the other side of the track near a town called Hummer, not far up the line from here. She challenged him to a race and suddenly took off running. The Flying Crow, forty-five minutes behind schedule, came roaring through at that moment and struck her. Streamliner usually stops the story there but you don't have to be a genius or an artist to imagine what the engine of that speeding train did to that little girl right before her brother's eyes. All he ever said was that they barely found enough of her to bury in the cemetery."

Birdie put his hands up on his ears. "Please, please, no details—no more."

"We've all got to talk about what happened to us, what we saw, what we did."

"That's even worse than what I saw, what happened to me."

"It made Streamliner sick. He couldn't get over it or talk about it—or anything else. I mean, he didn't say a word to anybody about anything from that day until he spoke to me one day here at Somerset, ten years later. Imagine not saying a word for ten years. There are several around here who've gone even longer, but they're mostly back in the incurables wing now. Anyhow, I was the one who finally got Streamliner to tell the story of what happened to him. Do you want to tell me what happened to you?"

Birdie shook his head. "No, thanks. Not now."

"All I'm saying, Birdie, is that you should talk to me—or to somebody else, if you want to—about what happened that causes you not to be able to close your eyes. That's all. Maybe it can help you the way it helped Streamliner to at least be able to say something—even if it's mostly only about trains."

Birdie started laughing. *Laughing.* "That's a really great idea," he said. "I can be an imaginary conductor on The Flying Crow? No thanks."

"At least he's functioning . . . more than he was before. Watch him. He walks around here all day calling out the names of towns, urging people to get on board, watch their step, have their tickets ready. He's always joyful, smiling, talking or shouting, always moving, always clicking an imaginary ticket punch or busy with the business of getting his train on down the track."

Birdie was still ignoring Josh. But that didn't stop Josh from talking.

"The bushwhackers mostly leave Streamliner alone. They and the doctors have figured that they have no better therapy to offer. They have no other way to help this tortured human being than to let him play conductor on the same train that ran over his sister. He mumbles himself to sleep every night, and that sure beats having a ball bat slammed against his head."

"I don't want to pretend I'm a conductor on The Flying Crow, for God's sake," Birdie said.

Josh would not quit. "They allow Streamliner a special privilege. Every Thursday morning he gets to go down the hill right next to the Kansas City Southern track and watch the northbound Flying Crow go by. The train always slows down when it gets to him, and he waves and shouts and the engineer blows his whistle—"

"You want to help *me,* get me a woman. I need women and they need me. All I need is to put my hands on a beautiful woman's tits for a few seconds and I'll be better. What about the women patients? Get me one of them."

Now Josh laughed. "Can't do that. No fraternization of any kind allowed. There are no women available here at Somerset for men patients to do what you want to do, Mr. Birdie of Kansas City. The only form of sex available is through—you know, doing it to yourself."

"That makes your hair fall out."

"If that were true, there wouldn't be anything but bald men around here."

They both laughed. It was the first time they had done that together.

"What happened to you, Birdie?" Josh asked quietly. "What did you see?"

"I'm not talking about it to anyone."

Amos and the other two bushwhackers returned. They helped Birdie out of the tub and gave him a large white towel to dry himself off, but they wouldn't let him wrap it around himself when he was finished. Naked, Birdie went with them and Josh down the hallway and into the ward.

Birdie did not cover his genitals. Adjustment to life at the Sunset at Somerset sometimes came remarkably fast.

Once in the ward, the bushwhackers made Birdie, still naked, climb into bed and lie on his back, and they tied him down again.

"Close your eyes," said Amos. "Let's see if the hot water calmed you down."

Birdie closed his eyes. His arms and legs immediately stiffened and he screamed, "Nooooo! Don't shoot no more! The blood! No, no!"

Amos raised his slugger to whack Birdie in the head from the right and another bushwhacker got ready to do so from the left, but before either took a swing, Birdie opened his eyes and went absolutely and peacefully silent and still.

 Lawrence of Sedalia's pleas and protests had become as much of the show as Josh and, as always, his noise and screams for mercy and deliverance were followed by other patients asking for the same. Streamliner, as always, was going about his business as a conductor, standing in an aisle and going through the silent motions of taking tickets and helping passengers board his train.

The bushwhackers let the racket from Lawrence and the others go on a few minutes, until it built to a small roar, and then stopped it short.

Amos the ass from St. Joseph came down to the front row and, with everybody watching expectantly, bashed a padded Somerset Slugger down across the top of Lawrence's head. That shut up Lawrence and the other noisemakers.

The sound of the baseball bat landing on Lawrence's head was Josh's cue. Now the show was really on.

Josh turned around to face his audience. Like magic, the look in his eyes and around his mouth was that of a little boy, a boy of about eleven or twelve. It was uncanny. How was he able to change his face that way? Who knows? From the face of a grown man to that of a little boy—just like that. Maybe it was the hair. His long dark-brown hair had disappeared under a large flannel white-and-black-striped baseball cap. Or maybe it was magic. Or maybe just acting.

In the high-pitched, squeaky unchanged voice of a boy, Josh said,

"I had gone to my grandmama's house that morning of September 27, 1864, to help her clean her cistern. Our little town of Centralia was in a wide prairie with barely a tree high enough to climb, which meant you could see from the roof of any building for miles around. We only had two hotels, a saloon, and two stores that sold dry goods plus our little train station. There were about twenty-five houses, only two of them two stories high. One of those was my grandmama's, and I liked to go up to the second floor and look out to see what there was to see, which usually wasn't much. But this morning I hadn't been up yet because I had a chore to do. Some cottonwood leaves and limbs had gotten down in the tank during a rainstorm a few nights before.

"I was outside on the north side of Grandmama's house when, out of the air like a bad breeze, came the voice of somebody yelling, 'Bushwhackers! Bushwhackers! They robbed the Columbia stage! They're all over town!' "

Josh smiled, cleared his throat, and began talking in his normal adult voice. He couldn't keep up that squeaking for the entire presentation, but he did stay in the first person, telling the story through the eyes of a boy in Centralia in 1864.

"I knew about the stagecoach from Columbia, a bigger town and our county seat, thirty miles south of Centralia. It came every day about this time, and I often watched it approach from the south from Grandmama's second floor.

"I raced around to the front of the house and saw little Willie Hooper running down our street raising dust. He was the one doing the hollering, so I immediately put any worries to rest on grounds that Willie, two years younger than me, was known for being afraid of his own shadow.

"But in a few seconds, coming up behind him in a huge cloud of flying dirt, was a man on a big black horse who was dressed all in black, too. He rode right on by Willie to me—to Grandmama's house.

" 'Breakfast, boy. I want some breakfast. You got some woman around in that big house here who'll fix me breakfast?'

"It was a little late in the morning for breakfast, was what I thought first. But then I looked closer at the man. I could tell he was evil. His look struck me as being a cross between a black crow and a gray rat. He had a thin mustache and dark brown hair that was long and thick and everywhere, falling like a prissy girl's over his ears, where it kept going into a wide beard that circled and covered the bottom part of his face before ending right in the center in a point. His hat, his shirt that looked velvet, his pants, and his boots were all black. That hat was wide-brimmed and made of felt and it had a star-shaped pin that held the brim against the crown in front. I had heard that the bushwhackers wore a star as a sign they were organized like soldiers. The star was silver, about the size of a lawman's badge."

Josh closed his eyes, lowered his head. There wasn't a sound in the auditorium. Even Lawrence of Sedalia was quiet.

Then Josh raised his head. His eyes were open, but now they were slightly squinted. "His eyes were cold like the ice across a frozen lake on a dirty gray day. I shivered from fear."

Josh saw Lawrence shiver and put his hands over his own eyes—as he always did at this part.

"Then I saw the pistols. There was one in a holster on each hip and two more stuck down in his belt in front. They were enormous, the size of axes.

" 'You ought to try the El Dorado Hotel, back the other way by the station, right in the center of town,' I said, pointing south. Like I said, what we had in our small downtown wasn't much, but there were places to eat.

"The man grabbed a pistol from his belt and pointed it right at me, right, it seemed to me, at a spot between my two eyes, both of which were at that moment filling with fear and tears. I was certain I was about to die. At age fourteen, my life was now ending. We all knew about the bushwhackers. I had heard they loved to cut off pieces of Union soldiers they had killed and keep them as souvenirs. What part of me would he chop off and display?"

Josh stopped and gave a slight pointed bow to the five or six Somerset bushwhackers, employees of the state of Missouri, who were standing around the auditorium in their white attendants' uniforms. Most of them seemed to puff up, to smile.

He continued, changing his voice back to the stiff, formal one with which he began. "The word bushwhacker according to the dictionaries is, quote, 'one accustomed to beat about or travel through bushes.' "

The 1933 bushwhackers of the Missouri State Asylum for the Insane again preened. They appeared to appreciate the definition even though, as one had said to Josh before, they mostly had no idea what it really meant. Why would people go around beating up bushes? Whacking patients in insane asylums made more sense.

Josh continued in his Centralia performance voice. "Their supporters around our town claimed they were only matching the Yankee soldiers' meaness and murder and savagery. My family was mostly neutral about the war, with my mother and father and uncles and aunts trying their best to stay out of it altogether. Only my grandmama took sides, and that was for the Union. I knew there was no way she was going to make a meal for a bush-whacker.

" 'I just came from the El Dorado, boy,' the bushwhacker said to me. His voice was as clipped and direct as his eyes. 'They got nothing there I want 'cept whiskey, which I've plenty of. Now come over here, boy, and get up be-hind me on this horse. You're going with me to find some breakfast.'

"The man extended his right hand down toward me. It was covered in a slick black leather glove. 'We don't kill women and children, boy, if that's what's got your mind occupied.' "

V

WILL

SOMERSET

1918

Will Mitchell, MD, came running to the infirmary in the basement of Old Main. An attendant had summoned him with the alarming news that a patient had tried to kill himself while working at the asylum's farm. Dr. Mayfield was seeing to him now. Randall Mayfield, MD, was the asylum's medical director and Will's boss.

But Will couldn't find anybody. Not only were the patient and Mayfield not around, neither was the duty nurse—at least, not in the treatment room or the operating room. There hadn't been time to get the injured man out of here to town to the local hospital in Somerset.

So where was everybody?

The infirmary consisted of four designated spaces, the largest being the treatment room, where the patients were routinely examined and their physical ailments seen to. The other two areas besides the operating room were the administrative offices and the autopsy laboratory.

The autopsy laboratory. Yes. That must be where they were. The poor bastard must be dead, and Mayfield, true to form, was wasting no time. Will hurried down the narrow hallway that separated the lab from the rest of the infirmary. As he went, he began to hear voices. That was it. The patient had succeeded in killing himself.

Will, the son and grandson of Kansas City doctors, had grown up around the unpleasantries of human death. They were part of his life long before he went to medical school at the University of Missouri at Columbia. So when he opened the door to the autopsy lab, he barely noticed the horrendous odors that immediately filled his nostrils. They were as routine to him as walking through snow was for a postman.

But there was something here that was not routine. The man laid out naked on the stainless-steel autopsy table in the middle of the room was not dead. It was Joshua Lancaster, a patient everybody called Josh.

Mayfield and a nurse, a sour woman named Ruth Jensen, were getting autopsy cutting instruments ready at another smaller table. Their backs were to the door and to the corpse—which was not a corpse at all. Will's eyes had gone right to the man's chest, which was scarred with five large bloody holes, the work, no doubt, of a farm tool of some kind. It didn't appear to Will that the wounds had been dressed or even cleaned.

But, more important, the chest was moving up and down in that slow rhythm associated with breathing—with being alive.

"What have we got here?" Will asked Mayfield, who turned around at the sound of Will's voice.

"We're preparing to take the brain for study," said Mayfield, as if announcing the page number of the next hymn in church. "It promises to be a most interesting specimen. You are welcome to assist, Dr. Mitchell."

"But, look—he's still breathing!"

"I know, but he soon won't be," said Mayfield, a tall, skinny, pinched man of fifty who—Will had come to believe—suffered from his own special kind of mental illness.

"There doesn't seem to be that much external bleeding or major trauma," Will said. "Shouldn't we do a little something to see if we can save him first?"

"It would be a waste of time and purpose," said Mayfield. "His use to society lies now in the extraordinary potential for what we can learn from the study of his brain."

Mayfield was obsessed with the brains of dead insane people. That was his sickness. He couldn't keep his hands and scalpels and theories off of lunatics' brains. Will understood that it was a peculiarity that had begun quite normally, and even quite professionally, out of a desire to discover the underlying causes of lunacy. Mayfield had concluded it was physical; the way cells of the brain developed and functioned was the answer to insanity. The task, then, was literally to track each and every one of those cells, identify those that cause people to commit specific types of violence and other acts of lunacy, and remove them as you would a tumor.

Based on nothing much more than instinct, Will had a hunch there was more to it than that. He moved over to Josh, the naked man on the steel table. He was unconscious. Will knew that Joshua Lancaster's symptoms were common ones. Something had happened to cause him to go mute and dysfunctional, to become unable to sleep normally or even to close his eyes without screaming bloody murder. The paperwork said, in fact, that a bloody murder was the cause of his insanity. Will hadn't had time yet to pursue the case beyond that.

Will picked up Josh Lancaster's right hand and felt his pulse. "It's weak, but steady," he announced, in a loud voice.

He placed the silver hearing valve of his stethoscope down on the man's battered chest and listened. "Heartbeat's still there," he said.

So. Here now for the first time—to Will's knowledge, at least—Mayfield's obsession with the brain had gone so far as to kill a man to get a particularly enticing one. Is that what was going on here?

"I'm sorry, Dr. Mayfield," said Will, without a second's hesitation. "I'm taking this patient back to the treatment room, and I'm going to make a run at saving his life."

Will had no idea how Mayfield, the man who hired him and had the power to fire him, would react. And, given his emotional state at the moment, Will didn't much care. He simply was not going to stand by while Josh Lancaster or any other patient was murdered for his interesting brain!

"I trust you are aware of the circumstances that caused this patient to be adjudged insane, Dr. Mitchell," said Mayfield. "Clues to the causes of his behavior that might be found in his brain cells could provide breakthrough findings of important dimensions."

"Fine. Then wait until he dies—really dies."

"*Wait.* That is a word, Dr. Mitchell, that has no place in our work, our search for answers to insanity. This man is clearly doomed to spend the rest of his life, no matter its length, in this institution as an incurable lunatic. I would remind you, also, that he is alive now only because he was adjudged to be insane. Otherwise, he would most surely have already expired unaturally at the end of a rope, hanging from a gallows in a public square."

Will didn't know about any of that. But whatever the consequences, he was going to prevent Joshua Lancaster's death on this day, at this time, by this method.

"I'm taking him out of here," said Will. Using a rubber sheet, he covered Josh up and pulled him off the autopsy table on to a wheeled wooden gurney.

Was Mayfield or Ruth Jensen going to make a move to stop him?

No. In what Will could only conclude was a sudden flash of sanity, Mayfield said, "All right, Dr. Mitchell. The patient is yours. For now, at least."

And Will wheeled Josh out of the room and back up the hall to the treatment room, where he began the work of saving a life.

VI

RANDY

KANSAS CITY

1997

Janice Leona Larson Higgins, former Harvey Girl. Randy knew from her write-up in "The Harvey Girls Menu" that Larson was her maiden name and Higgins came from Billy Higgins, a traveling book salesman she was married to for forty-five years. He died two years ago of prostate cancer. They had two married daughters and five grandchildren, all of whom lived in and around Kansas City.

It was with the help of an old railroad friend of his own family that Randy had located Janice through the Kansas City chapter of the Harvey Girls alumni club. There was a Janice with employment dates that seemed to match. So, after getting her address as well as her life story from the "Menu," the club's membership roster and newsletter, he went to see her.

"I'd like to talk to you about Birdie Carlucci," Randy said to the elderly woman after introducing himself—but only by name, no title. Nor did he say he was a police officer or show her a badge, justifying the omissions on grounds that he was not really on official police business.

She had answered his knock at the door of a small green-shingled house in the 6500 block of Holmes Avenue, in an old neighborhood off Troost in south Kansas City that once, to Randy's memory, was near the southwest limits of the city. Now, with its suburbs and interstates, the Kansas City metropolitan area sprawled hundreds of blocks—and miles—farther south, as well as way westward, over the line into Kansas.

"Birdie Carlucci? I'm not sure I know anybody—"

"From Union Station. He was at Union Station when you were a Harvey Girl."

"Birdie! Oh, yes. I never knew his last name," she said. "Birdie Carlucci. I never figured he was Italian. I've seen that name Carlucci somewhere, but not . . . oh, never mind." Her words were accompanied by a beaming smile.

Janice Higgins was very old but very well cared for. Her face was cracked and wrinkled but powdered almost white, her lips colored dark pink with precisely placed lipstick. Her white hair was cut short, perfectly combed, and held behind her ears with a dark blue ribbon. She was wearing a light-green housedress that was not only freshly pressed but also starched. She had had no idea Randy was coming to see her this morning. This was a woman who still lived her life in accordance with her training and habits as a Harvey Girl. Randy loved that—and her—as he had all Harvey Girls.

Janice Higgins invited him to come in, and he stepped into what was clearly her living room. There was no entrance hall or vestibule. It was a small house, probably built in the 1920s.

The cop in Randy wanted to warn this little old woman about the dangers of allowing strange men into her house like this. But as a cop on an unorthodox freelance mission of curiosity, he was delighted.

He declined her offer of coffee or tea but did sit down on a small blue-and-white flowered couch across a low table from her. She had gone to an overstuffed chair that was covered in a matching fabric. The set reminded Randy of a similar one—in red and white—in his own house. He and his wife, Melissa, had bought their set at Sears. Wonder where Janice Higgins got hers?

"Well, tell me about Birdie," she said in a sweet, open way. "I have often wondered what became of him. I lost track after I met Billy, got married, and left the Harvey House service. Billy was a traveling man. He came in one day for lunch when his train to Des Moines was late. Of course, that's how I met Birdie too. Is Birdie your father?"

Randy had come to ask questions, not answer them. But he said, "No, ma'am."

She was wearing large black-rimmed glasses but he had a good view through them of two bright blue eyes. They were focused right on him, too, waiting for him to say something. Your turn now, young man. If you're not his son, who in the hell are you? No, no. A Harvey Girl would never say *hell*.

"I only recently met Mr. Carlucci," Randy said, kicking himself for not having worked out in advance a good line of approach. He had just jumped in his unmarked police Chevy and driven out here, telling the various detectives in the office that he had to run an errand. "I'm on the box if you need me," he had said. That was not exactly true. He had left his handheld two-way radio in the car.

"I'm delighted to hear he's still with us," she said, her smile from the front door beginning to disappear. "My Billy died last year. He was the best salesman who ever worked for Zondervan—that's a religious book publisher. Billy had this territory for thirty years. He covered everything from Minneapolis south to Wichita, the Mississippi on the east and the Rocky Mountains on the west. He was gone a lot, but I got used to it."

She stopped and waited for a response. It was again Randy's turn.

He elected to stay on his subject, not her's. "I assume you knew that Birdie actually lived at Union Station," he said, deciding that he had to get on with it. And the truth—some of it, at least—was the way to go.

The smile began to return. "Oh, yes. He told me he had witnessed an awful crime somewhere but he didn't want to talk to the police and FBI about it because it involved some of his relatives—I think that's what he said. It was a long time ago. At any rate, that's why he stayed out of sight there at the station for a while."

A while? How about sixty-three years? Did she not know how long Birdie was there?

Randy held that thought to himself. "He told me you brought him food from time to time."

"That's right. We became good friends—in a way. Maybe in more than one way."

Randy thought he saw a quick flash of red appear under the white powder on her cheeks. Once a Harvey Girl, always a Harvey Girl.

"Do you ever remember meeting another friend of his, someone named Josh?"

She shook her head and looked off to an end table on the left at a large photo portrait of a man in a dark suit whom Randy figured to be Billy Higgins. "Josh," she repeated. "Frankly, I didn't realize he had any other friends around the station besides me. He kept himself washed, shaved, and neat and had nothing to do with the other men who hung out at the station. Birdie was no bum like they were."

"The Josh I'm talking about came with Birdie to the station the first time, I believe."

Her eyes brightened. "Oh, yes. There were two men with him the day I met Birdie. They came into the Harvey House for breakfast. There was an older man who had pancakes and a younger one who just ordered coffee."

Randy marveled at her ability to remember such details. But of course, she *was* a Harvey Girl. "Josh was the older one," he said.

"I was only with him and the other man for a short time. What do you want to know about him?"

"His last name. Did you hear—and remember—a last name?"

She thought again for a few seconds. Then, as if recalling something, she turned back to Randy. "I do remember something about the other man—the younger one. He was a doctor. His name was Mitchell. Yes, I'm pretty sure it was Mitchell. I know that because there were some big doctors in town then by that name—still are, for that matter."

Randy felt good. He had another name. His curiosity had somewhere else to go.

Common courtesy dictated that he stay and chat with Janice Higgins for another couple of minutes. But common sense told him to go. Who knows what might be squawking out of that radio on the front seat of his car.

So he said he had to go and rose to his feet.

She stood also. "You're a police officer, aren't you?"

Randy was certain she could see the red that was coming from the heat he felt in his cheeks. "Yes, ma'am, I am. I should have identified myself. I apologize."

"Are you people still trying to get poor Birdie to talk about whatever it was he witnessed those many years ago? That's it, isn't it?"

Randy just shook his head. He didn't know what she was talking about.

"That's really stupid, if it's true. Have you read that new book about the Union Station massacre Jules Perkins wrote? It amazes me the way people keep looking at things that happened years ago. I was working there at the station that morning, but I didn't see a thing except the commotion afterward. I can't believe J. Edgar Hoover would just make it up the way Perkins said. But I *do* love Perkins's novels. Don't you?"

Randy nodded his head to acknowledge he had read *Put 'Em Up!* and that he, too, enjoyed Perkins's other books. Most were high-action crime stories set in Kansas City in the seventies, and Randy had, in fact, read two or three of them.

"Well, if you see Birdie again, tell him 'Thanks for the Memories,' " said Janice Higgins. "That's Bob Hope's song. Birdie'll get it."

Randy promised to deliver the message.

He waited until he had turned the corner at Linwood Boulevard a block away before picking up the radio and checking in. There had been no emergencies, no important calls. Nothing had happened.

Except that he now had the name of Josh's doctor—and he had promised to say "Thanks for the Memories" to Birdie Carlucci.

VII

JOSH AND BIRDIE

SOMERSET

1933

It was ten-thirty in the morning and Sister Hilda Owens was at the library, prepared to read poetry by Vachel Lindsay and Henry Wadsworth Longfellow out loud.

"I could recite something else, of course, if you prefer," she said to Josh and Birdie, the only two patients who showed up. The reading was part of what the asylum called its Cultural Therapy Program. A bushwhacker had escorted them there and then left, telling Sister Hilda to "give a holler if they act up."

"How about this, Sister Hilda?" said Josh, handing her the library's copy of *John Brown's Body*.

They were in a quiet corner on the second floor of Old Main. Birdie and Josh, as the only attendees, sat across a long narrow table from Sister Hilda, as if they were in an office conducting some kind of interview. There were several other chairs set up around but nobody was in them.

"Certainly, Josh," she said, opening the book, while doing her best to avoid looking at Birdie, who, despite Josh's admonitions, was making a fool of himself.

He was lunging at Sister Hilda. Not physically coming up and over the table but by flicking his eyes, puckering his mouth, flexing his shoulders. It was embarrassing and stupid. If he had had a Somerset Slugger, Josh would have been tempted to whack Birdie along the side of the head.

"*John Brown's Body* by Stephen Vincent Benét," declared Sister Hilda, her eyes fixed on the book in front of her. "It's about the Civil War, isn't it? Yes, I'm sure it is. We read parts of it in high school. John Brown was an Abolitionist and he was hanged for treason."

"That's right," Josh said. "He led a raid against a federal arsenal in West Virginia."

"Harpers Ferry, I believe," said Sister Hilda.

"Yes, ma'am, that's correct. They said he was a lunatic, but who are we to say anything about that?" He smiled.

She laughed—pleasantly, personally, almost intimately.

Josh certainly didn't blame Birdie for lusting after this woman. Her laugh, like her voice, was as much a treat to listen to as her person was to look at. He had told Birdie that a Somerset Sister was like a hospital gray lady, but there was absolutely nothing gray about Hilda Owens. Her bright hair and silky skin and round lips shouted with color, as did the yellow-and-green flowered cotton dress she was wearing this morning. Josh figured her age at about twenty-five. She and her banker husband, who somebody said was at least fifteen years older, had moved to Somerset only a few months ago from Kansas City. Calling her Sister Hilda didn't seem right for such a pretty young woman. That name would better fit an ugly old woman in her fifties or sixties.

" 'Invocation' is the first section," she said. "That's where I will begin, right at the beginning. Is that what you had in mind, Josh?"

Josh said that would be splendid, thank you, ma'am.

Keeping her head and bright blue eyes down, she read:

> *"American muse, whose strong and diverse heart*
> *So many men have tried to understand*
> *But only made it smaller with their art,*
> *Because you are as various as your land,*
> *As mountainous-deep, as flowered with blue rivers,*
> *Thirsty with deserts, buried under snows,*
> *As native as the shape of Navajo quivers,*
> *And native, too, as the sea-voyaged rose—"*

"No! The blood! Don't shoot no more!"

Josh hammered Birdie hard on his head. "No more screaming now, no more!"

Sister Hilda had stopped her reading. "What's wrong, Josh?"

"This poor young man sees horror every time his eyes close. The poetry. . . . Well, it must have set him into a doze or something."

Birdie, eyes open now, was smiling at Sister Hilda. "That's right, ma'am. I am so sorry that my lunacy affected your beautiful reading of that story. I was having trouble following what was happening."

"It's not just a regular story. It's poetry. I thought you said the other day that you loved poetry," she said sternly to Birdie.

"I do, I do. But I have trouble sleeping because of my sickness, so I am always sleepy even though I can't go to sleep."

"That's the way I used to be too, Sister Hilda," Josh said, trying to be helpful. "It takes time for patients like us to work through their horrors. I am trying to help Birdie here deal with his. But he is a very bad case, as you can see."

She returned to the book.

"Swift runner, never captured or subdued,
Seven-branched elk beside the mountain stream,
That half a hundred hunters have pursued
But never matched their bullets with the dream—"

"The blood! No!"

Josh again hit Birdie, causing the young man's screaming to stop.

A bushwhacker appeared from behind Josh and Birdie. "You all right in here, Sister Hilda?" he asked. "I heard some yelling." The bushwhacker had a Somerset Slugger in his hands. He was a large, coarse, fairly old guy named Roger, who was known mostly for being mean and for being from Holden, up near Kansas City. Somebody told Josh he was hired because his mother was a second cousin of the superintendent, who was also from Holden. All the Somerset superintendents Josh had known or heard about had reputations not only for hiring their relatives and friends, but also for being political in most everything they did, including taking money for admitting particular patients.

"I'm fine," Sister Hilda told the bushwhacker. "Birdie here just had a bit of a poetry setback, that's all."

The bushwhacker left and Sister Hilda, clearly new to the frustrations that went with being a Somerset Sister, gave Josh a look that said, All right, Josh, what now?

"There is something you might do that could be of help," he said, his voice as peaceful and earnest as he could make it. "It's perfectly understandable if you would not want to do what I'm about to suggest. In fact, I think I probably shouldn't even suggest it, and I will understand perfectly if it annoys you that I have."

Josh did not even try to steal a glance at Birdie. He could hear and sense the kid from Kansas City panting after this woman.

Sister Hilda seemed to take a breath and hold it tight. It was if she knew she was about to hear something awful yet felt she had no choice but to hear it.

"One possible way to help Birdie would be if you would allow him to put his hands on your bosoms for a few seconds," Josh said.

Braced for the worst, Josh watched a burning red flash come to Sister Hilda's cheeks. Then, in a series of quick reactions, she jerked her head back and, her eyes popping, caught her breath.

Realizing all he could do now was to keep talking, Josh said, "He needs to do it for his therapy, Sister Hilda. He told me last night that if he could touch a woman's bosoms for a just a few seconds—to a count of ten or twelve, fifteen maybe—he might be able to go to sleep like a normal person. You know he hasn't really slept since he saw something awful happen—an awful massacre."

"What massacre? Where?"

"I'm not able to say what or where," Birdie answered. "It turns me completely crazy even to think about it."

Sister Hilda, her face color returning to normal, shook her head as if to clear it and looked back down at Stephen Vincent Benét's *John Brown's Body*. Josh, worried about having upset her so, turned his thoughts to poetry and to the poems of Longfellow and Vachel Lindsay. Josh hadn't read anything by either man since he came to Somerset. He would now. He would ask Sister Hilda to read their poems next time, just like she had planned to today. He wondered if there were still people out there in the world writing new poems. Josh, an avid reader of many genres, spent as much time as he could in the library, particularly at this table, reading Civil War and Missouri history.

"I know you're a sick man, Josh," said Sister Hilda, her composure and appearance both almost back to normal. "As a consequence, I will act as if I did not hear what you said and will not report you to one of the attendants or to the superintendent for discipline."

Josh figured there was no point in stopping now. "Sister Hilda, thank you. But if I may say one more thing. You know about culture therapy and hydrotherapy and the other things that are there to help us get well?"

She looked at him but didn't say anything.

Josh hung in. "What I'm suggesting is another kind of therapy. We had a very sick man in here from Springfield who hadn't spoken a word or walked a step since he killed a sheriff with a shotgun. One day the doctors worked it out for him to hug one of the dentist's nurses tight for just a minute or so and, presto, he shouted for joy and got up and walked away. He's been on the steady road to recovery ever since."

Hilda Owens, the Somerset Sister, moved her head slightly but avoided any eye contact with Birdie, the potential beneficiary of the proposition. She said, "What about the murder? The killing of the sheriff? What are they going to do about that, if and when he arrives at the end of the road to recovery—assuming he does?"

"They're going to take him back to Springfield and hang him," Josh said.

A frown crossed Sister Hilda's face. Was she imagining a man hanging?

"Did you murder anybody at your massacre?" she asked Birdie, suddenly turning to him and looking him in the eye.

"No, ma'am," he said, his face and body clearly full of anticipation. From Josh's view, Birdie, cleaned up soft and soapy from an hour of hydrotherapy, his black hair combed and slicked straight back, didn't look so bad. If the truth were known, Sister Hilda could do worse than have his hands on her bosoms.

"Then why are you in here?" she asked Birdie.

"Watching it made me crazy. I can't close my eyes or go to sleep without screaming from what I saw. All that blood and dying and awfulness always comes back."

"What happens to you if and when you're cured? I don't know about that man from Springfield, but they told me very few . . . I'm sorry, but they said only a few ever leave here really cured."

"That's right. That Springfield man's still here, as a matter of fact," Josh said quickly. "But I think our Birdie has a real chance—with the right therapy. He's still very young."

"I'd go back home to Kansas City if I was cured," Birdie added. "I might even try to get a job selling the *Kansas City Star*. My cousin did, and I would love to do that."

Sister Hilda looked up toward the heavens, as if asking for permission or forgiveness, and said, "All right, then, I guess it's the least I can do—particularly for somebody from Kansas City. That's where I'm from too."

She scooted her chair back from the table, stood, and motioned for Birdie to follow her into the book stacks.

Birdie followed her out of sight between two tall shelves of books, HISTORY (MISSOURI) on the left, FICTION (A–L) on the right.

Josh didn't have a watch or a clock and he had never been good at estimating or guessing time, but it seemed like almost ten minutes went by before he heard the first real sound. It was a male groan. Then a slight feminine chirp, a cooing. . . .

Obviously, something besides a few seconds of bosom-touching was happening back there among the books. Josh was overcome with shame for listening. He grabbed *John Brown's Body* and continued reading loudly where Sister Hilda had left off.

> *"Where the great huntsmen failed, I set my sorry*
> *And mortal snare for your immortal quarry.*
> *You are the buffalo-ghost, the broncho-ghost*
> *With dollar-silver in your saddle-horn . . ."*

Josh paused for just a second to take a breath. "Yes, yes, yes," said a soft female voice coming from the stacks.

> *"The cowboys riding in from Painted Post,*
> *The Indian arrow in the Indian corn—"*

"Oh, oh, oh," said a raspy male voice coming from the book stacks.

> *"And you are the clipped velvet of the lawns*
> *Where Shropshire grows from Massachusetts sods,*
> *The grey Maine rocks—and the war-painted dawns*
> *That break above the Garden of the Gods."*

Josh felt somebody next to him. It was Roger from Holden with his Somerset Slugger.

"Where's the lady and the other loony?" he asked Josh.

Josh shrugged. How would I know? he was trying to say.

Josh heard a male voice say, "Thank you, thank you, Sister Hilda." It was coming from the stacks. "I will carry this with me at all times—now and forever."

Unfortunately, Roger of Holden also heard it.

In a flash he disappeared, back between HISTORY (MISSOURI) and FICTION (A–L).

Josh flinched at the familiar sound of a ball bat hitting a human head—once, twice, three times—and Sister Hilda screaming, "No! Stop that!"

Josh stood up and ran into the stacks.

Birdie, his pants down around his ankles, was sitting against a bookshelf, his head being hammered from side to side by Roger's bat.

Sister Hilda, her stockings and underclothes also down around her shoes, was pulling at Roger from behind, sobbing, yelling, begging for the whacking of Birdie to stop.

Josh stepped forward to help her and immediately caught a blow alongside his own head that knocked him out cold.

"I had heard that before, but when he pointed his gun at me I had forgotten it. And it remained mostly forgotten. I figured I had no choice but to do what he wanted. It probably wouldn't be long before Grandmama saw what was happening through a window and came running out with a stick or a rock and some hot words.

"I peed my pants. I couldn't help it. It went down my leg and all over the front of my pants, which were brown cotton and tight and had been my cousin's before they were mine."

Lawrence of Sedalia let out a screaming, whooping, hysterical laugh. Another patient yelled, "The pee was scared right out of ya, little boy Josh, is that it?" It was the first break in the quiet that had held for the last few minutes. And after a couple of the bushwhackers gave the room some stern looks, quiet quickly returned.

Josh continued.

"I was humiliated and ashamed, but nobody but the bushwhacker could have seen what I did and I wasn't even sure he had. If he saw, he didn't say anything or seem to mind. How could he? I reached forward and let the bushwhacker grab my right hand. He jerked his right foot out of the stirrup, I replaced it with mine, and with a quick pull and a jump I was sitting up on the saddle behind him.

"I didn't want to touch him but I had to grab on to something to keep from falling off, so I took a handful of his coat in each of my hands and hung on. I could feel his back, his body, or least his black coat, through my wet pants, and I didn't mind that I might be getting him wet with my pee."

"Hooray for Josh's wet pants!" a patient yelled. "Three cheers for Josh's wet pants!" And, not unlike a school cheerleading squad, just about everyone in the auditorium, including even a couple of the bushwhackers, stood and screamed, "Hip, hip, hooray!" three times. Like Lawrence of Sedalia's outbursts of fear and laughter, that was part of the regular ritual of the performance.

When the cheering stopped, Josh went on.

"I tried to hold my breath to keep from smelling the bushwhacker but I couldn't do it for long. The first odor that hit me was the whiskey he'd been talking about having just drunk at the El Dorado Hotel. It was something I was most familiar with because of being a lot with my Uncle Luther, a big drinker. But the bushwhacker's stench was more mixed than that. Whiffs of spit and rotten food and gunpowder and people's dried sweat and what I imagined to be people's blood and guts also lodged in my nose and eased up into my brain and down into my throat. I figured if he didn't shoot me I was going to die anyhow of smell poisoning, that was for sure. So I was actually happy to have added some odor of pee to the occasion."

Again led by Lawrence of Sedalia, a few of the patients broke into loud, piercing laughter; others stomped their feet and rattled their chairs. When they didn't stop after a couple of minutes, Amos the Ass stood with the Somerset Slugger up over his head. That got the auditorium quiet again.

Josh moved right up to the edge of the stage.

You could actually hear the sucking sound as the roomful of patients and bushwhackers took a deep breath—all at once, as if on command. Most everyone knew what was coming next.

"My right hand slipped from the bushwhacker's coat. I grabbed for something else. I had hold of a thing that felt human, hairy. I peered around the back of the bushwhacker. I had a scalp in my hand! It was the top of the head of a human being, tied to the saddle horn. The hair was blond, matted in places with mud and blood. The skin underneath was shriveled. There were two, maybe three other scalps; one, maybe two ears; and four noses— all dried like prunes, tied by heavy black string."

Josh paused. He looked out into the audience, scanning from left to right, back to front. His eyes were met with those of his fellow lunatics, most of them opened wide and fixed on his.

Josh took two steps backward. "I wanted to vomit. My stomach and my throat and my spirit wanted to regurgitate. But I knew if I vomited on the back of the man's black coat he would kill me for sure. I closed my eyes, grabbed the coat again, and prayed silently to God in heaven to keep me from regurgitating myself to certain death."

Somebody down front broke the silence by gagging—loudly, horrendously—making the sound of someone on the verge of emptying his entire insides in front of everyone in Flynn Auditorium. This had never happened before. Vomiting by one of the patients—even Lawrence—was not part of the performance. Josh saw in a flash that it was a new boy. Welcome to life as a lunatic at Somerset.

Josh moved on with his story—quickly. "God answered my prayer. I was suddenly fine and no longer felt the impending need to regurgitate."

The gagging sound stopped. The new patient was quiet again. Maybe he too had successfully prayed to God to spare him a regurgitation.

"We were off toward town, the bushwhacker whomping his legs and boots hard against the belly of his horse. 'Grub time, Midnight!' he yelled. I assumed this was the name of the horse, a tall stallion with a coat that was blacker than any midnight I had ever known.

"We had barely gone a block—the whole town was no more than five or six blocks north and south, east and west—when two other fierce-looking men on horseback came riding up. Both of them had large tin cups of whiskey in one hand, their horses' reins in the other. 'Captain Bill, there's a train coming in from the east,' one of them shouted at my bushwhacker.

" 'It's all ours!' my bushwhacker yelled back.

"Captain Bill, they called him. I was sure from the way the others talked to him and his return shout that I was on a horse with the man in charge— some kind of chief bushwhacker, the head evildoer. His name was Bill, was all I knew, except that he reeked of meanness.

"What I also knew at the moment was that the approaching train had to be the Northern Missouri Railroad passenger run that came in every morning from St. Louis by way of St. Charles, Wentzville, Wright City, Warrenton, Wellsville, Jefftown, and Mexico.

" 'Jump off, boy,' said the bushwhacker to me. 'I got more serious things to do now than find some breakfast.'

"He slowed his horse down long enough for me slip down off the rear of the mount to the ground. He rode away without another word, and I started to turn and run back to Grandmama's house as fast as I could. But I couldn't move. There was too much to see, too much happening in and around me. I walked, not ran, downtown to a place alongside a house that was next to the El Dorado Hotel. I had no plan, other than to stand there, to hide there, to be invisible while I watched what neither God in heaven nor the Devil in hell could have imagined was about to unfold before my tortured eyes.

"What I saw first was more bushwhackers racing around on horseback in all directions, shooting their pistols up in the air and yelling insults at the citizens of Centralia, some of whom I recognized. I wondered why these good folks didn't get away and seek safety or protection. I heard some claiming to the bushwhackers that they were southern sympathizers and shouldn't have their property or person damaged. That struck me as pointless and stupid.

"Most of the bushwhackers were wearing blue Union soldiers' coats, which they had probably stolen off dead Union soldiers. They rode in twos or more. And then I heard one shout, 'We are Bill Anderson's men!'

"So! My bushwhacker was none other than Bill Anderson, 'Bloody Bill,' they called him, because he was known to be the most ruthless and notorious and inhuman of all the bushwhacker leaders. And I had just met him, rode on his horse with him. I couldn't believe it, fathom it, or digest it."

VIII

WILL

SOMERSET

1918

Josh regained consciousness. His eyes were open.

"Don't you think it's about time you started talking, Josh?" Dr. Mitchell asked.

Josh did not respond and showed no reaction in his face. It was as if he didn't hear the question.

"When was the last time you spoke a word to somebody—anybody?"

Again, no response.

They had been in the treatment room for less than ten minutes. Josh was still lying face-up on the gurney. Dr. Mitchell, assisted by two attendants, had washed the blood from Josh's chest wounds and was now covering the five gaping holes with large white cotton bandages.

"I take it you have a problem with living, is that right?" Mitchell said, in a friendly, casual manner.

Before anybody could stop him, Josh thrust his two hands down to his chest and ripped at the bandages.

The attendants gripped Josh's arms and after a few seconds of struggle held them down long enough for Dr. Mitchell to bind each to a side of the gurney with leather straps.

"So you really want to die, do you?" Mitchell said, once things had calmed down. The attendants also tied down Josh's legs. "Well, that's too damned bad, because I'm not going to let you."

The doctor waved his hand back and forth in front of Josh's face. There was no reaction. Josh stared straight ahead as if nothing were happening.

"Close your eyes, Josh. Let's see what happens when you close your eyes."

Josh not only did not shut his eyes, he opened them wider. From Mitchell's point of view, that was progress. Josh had finally reacted.

"I don't think you can keep them open like that for much longer, can you, Josh? You must be getting sleepy. You've had quite a day. Trying to kill yourself can be exhausting. What did you do, beat on yourself with a tool of some kind? That must have taken some doing and hurt like hell. Were you singing or reciting some poetry while you did it? Was it something by William

Shakespeare? As I remember, he wrote a lot of plays with great dying scenes in them. . . . Your lids are really getting heavy, aren't they? I'll bet they feel like they've got pieces of lead on them. It won't be long now before they'll be closed. Did your mother sing that go-to-sleep song to you? 'Go to sleep, little baby. Go to sleep, little baby. When you wake, your pretty pretty face . . .' "

The lids fell down across Josh's eyes.

One second passed. Two. Three.

His eyes popped wide open. So did his mouth.

"I'm sorry, I'm sorry! Please forgive me!"

Josh screamed so loudly, Dr. Mayfield and several nurses and attendants came running into the treatment room to see what was going on.

In a matter of a few minutes, it happened three more times. Josh's eyes fell shut, then sprang open to the accompaniment of screeches that were loud enough for God in heaven to hear.

Finally, at Mayfield's direction, one of the attendants put Josh to sleep with a whack to the head with a small piece of lead pipe and wheeled him away to an isolation room for the night.

"That's quite a life you saved him for, isn't it, Dr. Mitchell?" Mayfield said, once they were alone.

Will Mitchell, confused and upset, kept his mouth shut.

But Mayfield was not finished. "I would ask only that you consider one thing, Dr. Mitchell. How do you believe that man, had he been able, would have made the choice between continuing to live the way he is here now or making a contribution, through his death, that might speed up the desperately needed work on how to repair such severely damaged brains as his?"

Will Mitchell left the treatment room, the response in his head unspoken. He was more determined than ever to save the life of Joshua Alan Lancaster.

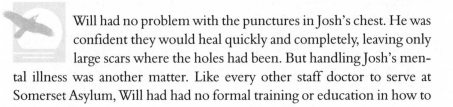 Will had no problem with the punctures in Josh's chest. He was confident they would heal quickly and completely, leaving only large scars where the holes had been. But handling Josh's mental illness was another matter. Like every other staff doctor to serve at Somerset Asylum, Will had had no formal training or education in how to

treat lunacy, much less cure it. It wasn't even in his curriculum at the University of Missouri School of Medicine in Columbia. He was only at Somerset because a doctor from the state health department happened to come by the St. Louis hospital where Will was finishing a routine general-medicine residency. The doctor was soliciting volunteers to come and "serve your community" for meager pay in one of the state hospitals. There was a particularly critical need in the state's five insane asylums, he said. Will had been headed since childhood for a comfortable slot in the well-established and prosperous downtown Kansas City practice of his father and three other partners. But Will, still unmarried and without other obligations, signed up to go to Somerset for two years. He figured, What the hell, why not? It might be an interesting experience, if nothing else.

He decided to treat Josh's sick mind during rocking time. It was a decision based solely on hunch and instinct rather than on any professional theory or research.

"Here's what we're going to do, Josh," said Will, the first afternoon. He had moved Josh and his rocking chair into a corner of the common room, as far away from the others as possible. "I'm not going to put on the straps and things. You can move, see, and talk. Got it?"

Josh smiled. He got it.

He was usually tied to the chair while he rocked back and forth, back and forth: *bump . . . ta, bump . . . ta.* He was also often gagged and blindfolded, with strips of tied or wadded-up white cotton cloth. The restraints on his movements, mouth, and eyes were a treatment designed by one of Will's predecessors a couple of years before. The idea was to force Josh to deal with the darkness and the fits that ensued without doing harm to himself or disrupting the peace and quiet of the other rockers, his fellow patients. The hope, based on nothing as far as Will could tell, was that eventually something would click in his diseased mind to end the fits.

Will's approach was also based on nothing but hope.

He said to Josh, "I want you to rock and rock while you tell me what you remember. I want you to begin at the beginning and go through every detail of what happened to you that caused you such pain and suffering then and continues to now. Got it?"

Josh began rocking. His shoulders shook slightly. He got it.

"Stay calm, Josh. Start with something small. The weather, maybe. Was the sun shining? Was it raining? Or was it dark—at night. Was there a wind blowing? From what direction? That kind of thing."

Nothing.

"Give me one tiny detail, only one. That's all you have to do. What were you wearing? Tell me that."

Josh kept his eyes open, staring straight ahead, and his mouth shut. The shaking spread to his hands, which were clutching the arms of the chair.

"The time of day. Just tell me what time it all started. Close your eyes and tell me if it was six o'clock or ten o'clock or whatever. Give me the time of day, Josh. Close your eyes."

Josh closed his eyes.

Will held his breath, his hope. He wondered if maybe he was the crazier of the two. He had no idea if this approach held out even a remote possibility of helping this man. Was it unethical or even illegal for a regular doctor to practice lunacy doctoring without a license or certificate of some kind? If it wasn't, it probably should be.

"Please, please forgive me! I'm so sorry!"

The piercing screech of Josh's scream brought two bushwhackers running into the common room and set off, like dominoes, talking and sobbing by several of the other patients.

Josh was quickly tied to his chair with leather straps, and cotton strips were put over his eyes and into his mouth.

Will told Josh he would be back to try again tomorrow.

Josh just kept on crying.

IX

RANDY

KANSAS CITY

1997

The doctor was cordial over the phone when he agreed to meet with Randy. But the next morning, sitting across a desk in his private office, Dr. William Bernard Mitchell III projected not even a hint of cordiality. He was polite, but the accompanying coolness made it clear this man did not want to talk about his father and the Somerset Asylum.

Something must have happened since Randy's call.

Yesterday, after some careful talk with a telephone receptionist in the medical offices of Mitchell, Mitchell and Barnes, Randy had determined for sure that he had the right Mitchell family. Then, when the physician came on the phone, Randy identified himself as a cop and said he'd like to discuss his father's work on a particular case at Somerset many years ago. Without a beat, the son said no problem. There was an old file of his father's around someplace with a lot of notes from back then. They set up an appointment for eleven next morning.

It was obvious now that what had happened overnight had to do with what was now lying on the desk in front of Dr. Mitchell: a thin faded dark-green cardboard file folder, which to Randy seemed of a style and design many years old.

"What is the law enforcement interest in my father's Somerset service?" said Dr. Mitchell. Randy estimated his age at about forty, his intelligence and diligence at A-plus. His face was tanned, his hair thinning brown, his build solid: all in all, a person of substance, somebody you would want in the operating room or at your bedside.

"We're trying to close out some old cases," Randy answered. "It's an efficiency move by the chief." Unlike his approach with the ex–Harvey Girl, he had worked out a line to use this time. He didn't want to lie but he also didn't want to leave empty-handed.

Randy couldn't tell from the doctor's facial expression if he bought that or not. The office walls were full of photographs of doctors in white coats who looked like this man. Randy wondered which was his father. Which was the friend of Birdie's friend Josh?

"What exactly is the crime that is alleged to have occurred in this matter?" said the doctor.

On impulse, Randy said, "That, in fact, is the purpose of our investigation. We are trying to identify the crime—if, in fact, there was one."

It didn't work. Dr. Mitchell looked away at something on the wall behind Randy, down at the closed file, and then back at Randy. "My father wrote a scathing indictment of what he witnessed—and participated in—during his very brief stay at Somerset Asylum. But from what I can tell he did nothing about it, showed it to no one, took no action. He merely wrote down his thoughts and recollections and put them in this file."

Crunch time. "I guess the bottom line, doctor, is, may I read the file?"

"No, you may not." He spoke with the casual firmness he might have used if he were telling a patient that he had an incurable disease.

"Why not, if I may ask?"

"Why should you, if *I* may ask?"

"Maybe there's something there that might help me identify . . ."

"Identify whom?"

"A patient named Josh. That's all I know about him. I know his first name, and the fact that your father—it must definitely have been your father—helped him in some very dramatic way at Somerset."

Dr. Mitchell opened the file and read the first page, turned to a second, and finally to a third.

"There is a name in here that may be the man you have in mind. The name is Joshua Alan Lancaster."

Randy wrote that down in a spiral notebook he quickly retrieved from a coat pocket. "What does it say about him?"

Dr. Mitchell closed the file and stood. "That's all I'm going to tell you, Lieutenant. The rest is protected by the doctor-patient relationship."

Randy, feeling forced also to be firm, said, "Whatever relationship your father had with Joshua Alan Lancaster was more than sixty years ago, doctor. And it was in his capacity as an employee of the state of Missouri."

"If you want more, get a court order. I'm sorry."

End of interview. OK. But Randy wasn't going to leave without asking one last question. "What's the problem, doctor? What kind of stuff is in there that you don't want anybody to know about sixty years later?"

"It's a simple matter of the right to privacy, Lieutenant."

"Whose privacy?"

"My father's."

Randy left the office, his hands still burning with the suppressed urged to swipe that file from the doctor's desk and make a run for it.

Maybe there was another way. Maybe there was an old retired burglar around who could be enticed to do a little black bag job. . . .

Yeah, yeah, yeah. Shame on you, Benton.

He smiled at the prospect of a big black headline in the *Star:* POLICE LIEUTENANT FIRED IN MEDICAL OFFICE BURGLARY LINKED TO LUNATIC, UNION STATION MASSACRE.

Then he looked at the bright side. He did have the full name of Birdie's friend: Joshua Alan Lancaster.

All right, Aunt Mary, time to do your stuff.

His aunt Mary was the only person around who still called him Randolph. She said it was because that was who he was the day he was born and that was who he would always be—to her, at least. *Randy,* she said, was the name of a high school kid, a college student, and, now, a Kansas City cop, but not of her nephew.

That was his aunt Mary. She was always slightly out of step with the rest of her family. *Peculiar* was the word her older brother, Randy's late father, used to describe her. He said—always with affection—that her pecularity was one of the reasons she was such a great librarian.

"I need your help on something concerning the Centralia massacre," Randy said. He had decided to telephone her while she was at work at the library so she wouldn't be able to turn it into a marathon call. Aunt Mary was a talker. He also thought it might be possible for her to put a finger on the information right there while he waited.

"It happened in 1864 and it was a nightmare of a slaughter, I can tell you that, Randolph," she said.

"I'm looking for a particular person—he would have been a kid—who was there—"

"My word, Randolph," she interrupted. Randy knew there was an Aunt Mary hit coming. She liked to tell funny stories and play jokes on people. And she was as much a laugher as she was a talker. She loved to laugh, to make others laugh. "I'm quite surprised that the Kansas City Police Department is still working on the case. What year is this, 1997? My word, I'd have sworn the case of the Centralia massacre was solved back when it happened, one hundred and thirty-three years ago. I'm sure I read in a book we have right here in our own little library that numerous eyewitnesses identified the main culprit as a man named Anderson, Bloody Bill Anderson, and they caught him a few weeks after it happened and executed him rather brutally on the spot, without benefit of trial or due process. Didn't you big-city detectives get the word there in Kansas City?"

And she laughed in her infectious way that Randy, as a kid, used to relish hearing. It was catching; it was almost impossible to be around Aunt Mary when she was laughing and not start laughing yourself.

"Very funny, Aunt Mary," he said, trying not to break up. Her laugh still had that effect on him.

Aunt Mary had been part of Randy's life since the day he was born in Winston, the railroad town forty miles east of Kansas City where all the Bentons came from. One of his father's brothers, Uncle Ted, who became a pharmacist in Kirksville, was the first of the Benton men not to work for the Missouri Pacific, which had a large engine and car overhaul yard in Winston. Randy was the second. The Benton women mostly married Missouri Pacific men because they were the only men around to marry. Aunt Mary, always the maverick, went off to what was then the state teachers college in Warrensburg, where she found her husband. He—Uncle Harold—was a star football player who became the high school coach in Langley. Aunt Mary, who earned a degree in education, went to work for the Langley library, while raising three kids, and had been there ever since.

"What do you need to know, Lieutenant Benton and, as they say in Washington, why do you need to know it?" asked Aunt Mary, ready now to do business.

"How do you know what they say in Washington, Aunt Mary?"

"Because I know how to read, Randolph. There are books and newspapers and magazines, right here in our tiny library even, that have just about everything that a person needs to know. Knowing what they say in Washington is crucial for all of us. How else can we understand what our leaders are telling us?"

Randy smiled, mentally kicking himself for taking her on—even in jest.

"I want to know about a kid named Joshua Alan Lancaster," he said, moving on. "He was an eyewitness to the massacre."

"Centralia is only about ten miles from here, as you know, but it's in Boone County," said Aunt Mary, moving on with him.

"But I figured you'd know how—"

"I'm doing it now," she said. Randy heard in the background the sound of computer keys being hit rapidly.

He kept silent.

"Nope, not there," she said, after a couple of minutes. "Let me try something else."

The computer noise resumed.

"Not there either." Aunt Mary paused. Randy assumed she was thinking. She was. "I have one last possibility."

She and her information machine completed one more search a few moments later.

"Nothing, Randolph." She spoke with finality. "The Boone County birth records show no Joshua Alan Lancaster or any name even close to that. The census records also have nothing. Most important, neither does a list the Boone County historical people have of every person who lived in and around Centralia at the time of the massacre. Your person wasn't there, Randolph. How old would he have been at the time?"

"Around fifteen, something like that."

"Well, like I said, there's no record of his being there in 1864 or at any other time. Now, Randolph, *my* question, please. Why do you need to know?"

In brief form, Randy told her about Birdie and his story of having come to the Union Station in 1933 with his friend Josh, who had witnessed the Centralia massacre.

"Have you put the dates and the supposed ages to a piece of paper, Randolph?" she asked, when he was finished.

"No," he confessed.

"Well, I just did while you were talking. The numbers don't quite add up. Your boy Josh most probably couldn't have been in Centralia. He would have had to be in his eighties in 1933 when he came to Union Station. That's not likely."

Randy was glad Aunt Mary could not see his face. She would have noticed—and commented on—the tinge of red that had come to his cheeks. That was another of his traits. It went with his temper.

"You never were good at mathematics, Randolph, and it appears you still aren't," she said, in her kidding way. "Thank the good lord you went into police work like your father, where deduction and confession can replace addition and subtraction."

Thank you, Aunt Mary. I love you, Aunt Mary.

Now she wanted to get caught up on family. How were Melissa and the kids? Randy reported his wife to be just fine, working part-time as a personnel consultant for a Kansas City insurance company. Mark, eight, and Joanie, six, were also well, flourishing in school and otherwise.

Randy was anxious to get on with it. Doesn't she have to get back to her library duties? Doesn't anybody in Langley need the assistance of their librarian? Won't somebody walk in off the street and ask for a particular book that can only be found by his aunt Mary?

Finally, he said, "Got to go, Aunt Mary. A policeman's work is never done."

"Yes, Randolph, I understand," she said in her special way. "I must say I am most puzzled about why you care about that man who lived in the Union Station building for so long. Although you were always so—so curious."

"You remember what Dad said, Aunt Mary?"

"I know, I know. 'Curiosity may kill the cat but it makes the cop.' "

They had one last laugh together before saying good-bye.

Randy barely took a breath before getting on the phone to an old contact—a sergeant named Rob Simmons—at the state police records division in Jefferson City. He asked for a criminal record check on a Joshua Alan Lancaster of Boone County.

Within minutes, Simmons was back with the word that there was only one entry for a Joshua Alan Lancaster. It was not from Boone County but from Baxter County, down in the southwest corner of the state, near Joplin.

"Whatever he did, it was over seventy years ago," Simmons said.

"Whatever he did? Doesn't his rap sheet state the offense?" said Randy.

"Nope. He was a juvenile. The file was sealed by some judge, and I'd guess that it remains sealed to this day in a courthouse basement."

Randy tried to think if he knew anybody in Baxter County or somewhere close by who might be prevailed upon to rustle through some old records. . . .

"The sheriff down there owes me one," Simmons said. "I'll see what I can shake loose. If something turns up, I'll have it sent to you."

Randy heaped thanks on Simmons, realizing that he now really owed Rob one.

This kind of thing was the subject of another of his dad's police truisms. "The only debts an honest cop should owe are to another honest cop."

X

JOSH AND BIRDIE

SOMERSET

1933

That smack of the bat from Roger of Holden was the only one Josh received. He was taken back to the ward, where he finally woke up. He managed to get through the rest of that day and the next without receiving any further punishment for his role in what happened in the library.

The punished ones—the victims—were Birdie and Sister Hilda.

Josh ached with guilt to the point of nausea and often felt like crying real tears for Hilda Owens. He, Josh, had ruined her life. His enticing this wonderful woman into doing something sexual as "therapy" was an outrageous assault on her giving nature. He could only imagine what her husband was doing to her. Do bankers just divorce wives who are unfaithful? Do they hit them with baseball bats? Or shoot them? Does it make any difference if the unfaithfulness was with a teenage lunatic who witnessed something terrible? Does that make it better or worse?

All Josh knew for sure about Sister Hilda was that Roger of Holden gleefully reported her to his relative, the superintendent, who immediately and publicly—at the asylum and around town—banished Hilda Owens for cause from the Somerset Sisters. Josh was told by another bushwhacker that nobody had seen Hilda Owens since she ran out of Old Main in tears. "Maybe her husband'll grab her by the hair and drag her back out here and lock her up in Beech," said the bushwhacker, and he laughed and laughed.

Josh knew he couldn't help Hilda Owens. She was condemned to whatever fate his own stupidity and thoughtlessness and her husband's anger generated.

But he could try to save Birdie.

Birdie's mind, if not his life, was in serious danger. Josh was sure of that. Nobody's head, not even that of a kid, could survive long under the kind of constant battering it was now going to get from Somerset Sluggers. Josh could remember over the years at least four patients who died after a few weeks of it. Several others were rendered permanently senseless and then taken behind the locked doors of Beech, never to be seen again. Josh had been friendly with one of them, a former high school teacher and football coach who, like Josh, loved to read and talk about early Missouri history. His certified proof of lunacy on the outside was that he preferred men—most specifically boys on his football team, unfortunately—to women. His punishable sin inside the asylum had been to expose himself in a gross way to one of the bushwhackers, whom he mistakenly believed shared his sexual preference.

Josh concluded there was only one thing he could do to protect Birdie: get the kid away from here. Maybe back to Kansas City, where he said he came from. Wherever, Birdie had to leave the Sunset in Somerset.

The way to do it came to Josh that evening after the violence in the library.

Three bushwhackers brought Birdie back to his bed minutes before lights-out, carrying him like a limp sack of something from a feed store. Birdie's head was drooping, his eyes were half-closed, his arms and legs dangled. There was no telling how many times he had been hit. Josh had not seen him at all, not even during the two periods of rocking time or pushing a broom in the hallway or in the dining hall.

After Birdie was strapped down in his bed and the lights went out, Josh went over to him.

"Can you hear me, Birdie? Can you talk? How are you?"

As if in a trance, Birdie shook his head but said nothing.

"Do you want me to get you out of here?" Josh whispered.

Birdie nodded.

At that moment, Josh heard Streamliner doing his quiet nightly call. "May I have your attention, please. This is your last call for The Flying Crow. All aboard for going straight as the crow flies to Hummer, Kansas City, and points north. Have your tickets ready, and watch your step while boarding the train."

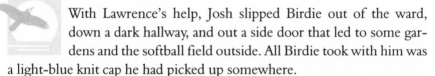With Lawrence's help, Josh slipped Birdie out of the ward, down a dark hallway, and out a side door that led to some gardens and the softball field outside. All Birdie took with him was a light-blue knit cap he had picked up somewhere.

The door to their ward was always unlocked just before six every morning, in case there were patients who needed to go the bathroom before official wake-up time came at six-thirty. Josh knew the bushwhackers, who worked twelve-hour shifts, were occupied with changing the night shift to the day shift. That happened every day at 6 A.M., no matter what.

At precisely 6:17, as on every Thursday morning, the outside door opened again and out walked Streamliner, carrying a wooden kitchen chair. His special privilege had become so accepted he was allowed to go alone through this door, across the ball field, and down Confederate Hill through the high-wire fence via a gate that he was given a key to unlock. Josh knew the procedure because he had helped work it out with the bushwhackers years ago and, in the beginning, even accompanied Streamliner several times on his rendezvous with The Flying Crow.

This morning, Josh, Birdie, and Lawrence were waiting in the darkness at the edge of the ball field. Birdie was still fairly weak from the beatings, but a night of sleep had renewed some strength. He could walk steadily and talk coherently, but maybe not think too clearly, it seemed to Josh, because the kid stopped cold when Josh said they were going to Kansas City on the train.

"Union Station? I can't go to Union Station," said Birdie. "They'll be looking for me. Everybody's been looking for me."

Looking for him for what? Josh was sympathetic. Maybe the poor head-whacked kid wouldn't go any farther. What could possibly be the harm in going to a train station?

But in a few seconds Birdie mumbled something about having no choice. He pulled the cap from a pocket, crammed it down on his head, and started walking again.

Josh was glad he had convinced Lawrence to help him this morning. It was only after Josh promised to fake laryngitis to avoid doing his Centralia massacre act for a while that Lawrence agreed to participate. Everybody has his price—even in lunatic asylums.

As he walked across the ball field, Streamliner was announcing to imaginary passengers that Somerset was the next stop. Josh, Birdie, and Lawrence fell in behind him on the path down the hill, staying out of sight. Once Streamliner had unlocked the gate, they followed and watched him place his chair down by the track.

Then, in accordance with Josh's motions, they moved to the left, to the south, away from Streamliner to where the end of the train was likely to be when it slowed down.

Just a few minutes later, they heard the roar of an approaching train. The Flying Crow was right on time at 6:43.

Several seconds passed before she actually appeared, her huge engine's headlight swinging back and forth across the track, her bells and whistles sounding, steam pouring up from under the wheels. Trains, particularly their locomotives, always struck Josh as being almost human. They seemed to have smiles or frowns on their faces, depending on their moods. The Flying Crow seemed happy this morning.

With Birdie and Lawrence, Josh moved down to the track. There were five, six, seven cars behind the engine.

The train was barely moving.

"Union Station, Union Station, I love Union Station," said Birdie, his voice high, full of fear. "But they might catch me if I don't watch out."

Josh felt sorry for the kid. He had seen a lot of patients at Somerset who kept thinking there were people or bugs or animals everywhere trying to get them. There was clearly more wrong with Birdie than he had realized.

Somerset was a flag stop, meaning The Flying Crow, after its almost twenty-four-hour trip up from Texas, only came to a full stop here if there were passengers known to be getting on or off. But on Thursday mornings, even if it didn't stop, it always slowed to a crawl, as it was doing now. One of the Somerset Sisters had managed to arrange that through somebody in town who knew an executive of the Kansas City Southern. It became KCS management policy to pay their respects to the man on the hill who was made a lunatic by The Flying Crow eighteen years ago.

"Slow to five miles an hour at the Big F Crossing at Hummer!" Josh heard Streamliner yell at the engineer and the firemen in the engine, which was just now arriving in front of him.

Streamliner's warning, Josh knew, was about the location, only twenty-one miles up the track from Somerset, where his sister was killed.

There was an answer from the train: two blasts of the whistle.

Josh, Birdie, and Lawrence were huddled opposite the end of the train, near the rear of the observation club car, which had an outside platform covered with an ornate canopy and a lighted electric foot-and-half-wide round red, yellow, and black sign. There was a black crow in flight painted in the center of the sign with the words THE FLYING CROW in a circle around it.

Josh and Lawrence helped Birdie climb up and over onto the platform. Birdie didn't need much help. He was able to pull himself up and swing his legs over. And then, with the train still moving slowly, he reached back and down toward Josh.

"Come with me, Josh," Birdie pleaded. "You're saner than anybody here—me included."

"I can't. I have to stay . . . I have no choice."

"Well, just ride with me to Union Station this morning. I'll tell you the story of the massacre I saw. I'll go through it, act it out. You have to help me. I won't know what to do without you."

Josh heard the whistle blow. The train was beginning to pick up speed. And in a flash of real lunacy, he let Birdie pull him partway onto the train platform—and then Lawrence gave a final push from behind.

Only Birdie was supposed to go. Only Birdie was to head straight as an arrow to Union Station at Kansas City.

Josh couldn't do this. Josh couldn't run away from Somerset. There were *real* people who would try to catch him.

I just stood there and watched the bushwhackers, Bloody Bill Anderson's men going crazy taking everything they wanted from people and from stores, the depot, and the saloons. If they wanted it, they grabbed it and cussed when they did.

"What they didn't steal they destroyed, cracking glassware and plates and cups by throwing them at walls and fences. They swaggered and staggered around and up and to and away from a barrel of whiskey someone had rolled out into the middle of the street. They helped themselves to the whiskey with tin cups. I saw one bushwhacker take a boot from a pair he had just stolen from someplace and force a man, a citizen of our town, to drink whiskey from it. I knew him to be a man who normally didn't drink whiskey because he thought it was the Devil's juice.

"Our town had become the Devil's town. I thought that my grandmama would be mad as the Devil himself if she'd seen what I now saw, which was one of those awful men as he unrolled a bolt of bright red-and-white checkered cloth while racing his horse down the street. Other horses came behind on top of that cloth and stomped into the dusty street it and all kinds of ribbons and other things that had been rifled and tossed out from stores like it was trash.

" 'The train! The train! Yonder comes the train!' one of the bushwhackers yelled.

"I looked toward the east and saw a line of black smoke coming. The bushwhacker drunks went into an even wilder frenzy, leaping on their horses and rushing toward the depot, where some were already throwing rails and ties on the track.

"In just a few minutes, I could see the train itself off in the distance coming, it seemed to me, at top speed as if it had no mind to stop in Centralia. The fool bushwhackers feverishly kept stacking rails and ties on the track. I figured the brakeman must have seen the barricade because the train suddenly started slowing down. Here it came down the track toward the station, accompanied by a piercing sound of scraping metal. The wheels were still turning, but it was obvious the brakes were on. As if God were in the cab, the train's five cars came to a halt right at the depot, the engine just a few feet away from the deadly barricade the fiends had constructed. It was a miracle.

"The bushwhackers blasted their pistols at the train cars. I could see pieces of glass and wood come down on the passengers inside. One of the cars seemed to be filled with men in blue coats. I wondered if they could be Union soldiers? If so, why weren't they firing back? Maybe I was seeing things. Maybe they weren't soldiers. Above the noise of the bushwhackers' pistol fire I could hear women and children shrieking for God, if no man, to help them.

"Soon the firing stopped, most of the bushwhackers dismounted, and, led by the man in black I now knew to be Bloody Bill Anderson, boarded the train. In the express car, the agent, confronted with pistol muzzles in his face, handed over the keys to the safe. I saw him give them away.

"More than a dozen men joined Anderson in the baggage car, clawing like animals at the luggage, trunks, and boxes. Was there cash money in there? I assumed there was and these villains were stealing it all!

"Other bushwhackers scrambled into the passenger cars and wrenched money, jewels, and anything else they liked from the terrified people who, by chance and bad luck, just happened to pick this day to ride this train. Oh, what can one say about fate? What if they had decided to make their trip tomorrow—or yesterday? They would have missed this tragedy. Some of the fiends even robbed children of their toys, which they then stomped to pieces. For what purpose? What threat did a child's teddy bear pose to Anderson and his band of bloody brothers?

"In the car of the bluecoats—I was now convinced they were soldiers—I watched with amazement as they all raised their hands above their heads.

"I was not the only citizen of Centralia watching this terrible show. People, mostly men and boys, were in windows or in corners, like me. I am reluctant to admit even now that at those early moments I felt an exciting rush of blood through me. It was a drama, horrible and hurtful, yes, but a drama of a level beyond anything any of us in our little Missouri town could ever have dreamt of witnessing."

Josh stopped talking and looked up at the ceiling of the auditorium, as if asking a benevolent God to hear his confession and forgive the sin of his excitement. Most everyone in the auditorium followed his lead in raising their heads to the heavens. They always did at this moment in the performance. It was a crucial step before moving on to the worst.

"Then, back out in front of the train, Anderson ordered all the passengers, except the soldiers, out and onto the platform. I still wondered why they had not fired at the bushwhackers, why they had not resisted. A man who worked in one of the stores, who was hiding near me, said they must be unarmed, probably on their way home on furlough. I was later to learn that that was, in fact, the case. There were only two pistols among all the soldiers, many of them on their way to Iowa and elsewhere west. So they had nothing with which to deter the bushwhackers. I regretted my bad thoughts about them."

Again, Josh looked at the ceiling. And again, his audience did the same.

"The soldiers were then told to leave the train on the other side. I and, I daresay, many other citizens of Centralia, moved to positions from which to see the sight.

" 'Take off your uniforms! Strip!' the bushwhackers yelled at the soldiers. They unbuttoned their jackets, removed their shoes or boots, pulled off their pants, and some, in their panic to please, even their underwear. I had never seen so many naked men at one time in my life. Their skin was all white and shivery. Was it possible to be scared out of your skin? Maybe so; maybe that's what I was seeing.

"I counted them. There were more than twenty. Twenty-one . . . twenty-two . . . twenty-three . . . twenty-four. And on to twenty-seven. Twenty-seven naked, humiliated, terrified men, some of them trying their best to hold their hands over their private parts. There were many people watching them—most of them men and boys like me. But there must have been women in windows of houses and the hotels and there were women and children passengers from the train who, if so inclined, could have stolen looks from between the train cars and other vantage points.

"Anderson, in a voice that the Devil himself would have admired, had the station and the boxcars on the siding set afire. Then he told the soldiers to form a single line across the street. I could tell that these men knew their fate. Some seemed to accept death. Some closed their eyes and moved their lips. I assumed they were praying. I wondered what kind of prayer made sense at a moment like this. 'Forgive me, God, for all my sins before I die?' Or, 'Promise me, God, never to forgive these awful fiends for what they're about to do to me.' "

Josh paused for a second and then said to the auditorium, his fellow patients and their watchers, "Which one of these prayers would you have prayed?"

Somebody yelled, "Never forgive them!" Then a couple of others screamed, "Forgive me!" And the room soon was divided almost evenly between those shouting "Never forgive them" and "Forgive me."

By this time in the performance, Josh no longer needed the bushwhackers and their Somerset Sluggers to maintain order. He let the thunderous noise of the competing shouts go on for a couple of minutes and then, with the raising of his right hand, shut it down and returned the auditorium to silence—and to his story.

"Other soldiers, instead of praying, sobbed and begged for their lives. 'I'm too young to die!' one cried out. He looked to be seventeen or eighteen, not much older than I was. It made me wonder just what was the proper age for death at the hands of Bill Anderson and his drunken bushwhackers. I felt sorry for the young soldier and the others, but I also was ashamed for them. They were soldiers of the United States. They should not have been acting this way—even if they were naked, even if their pubic hair and privates were exposed, along with their fear of a horrible death."

Josh fell silent. The auditorium remained silent. It was not possible to read that silence as the crowd being either in agreement or disagreement. Silent was what everyone was supposed to be right now, and they were all behaving as expected.

"The pleas of the men to be spared were answered by vile profanity from the bushwhackers with words I cannot repeat."

"Do it! Repeat them! Do it!" Several of the patients yelled. Josh expected it. Somebody called out.

Josh smiled and waved them quiet.

"They then herded the soldiers over to the front of the store. Two soldiers refused to move. Anderson immediately shot them dead. I mean, he fired at one with a pistol in his right hand, the other with a pistol in his left hand. The shots hit each in his forehead.

"Once the line was formed, one of the bushwhackers asked Anderson in a voice loud enough to be heard by everyone in town and, maybe, in the whole state of Missouri: 'What are we going to do with these fellows?'

" 'Parole them, of course,' Anderson yelled back.

"And the bushwhacker laughed heartily. 'That's what I thought you had in mind.' "

XI

WILL

SOMERSET

1919

There was a handwritten note on Will's desk when he arrived at the asylum one morning. He had assumed something like this would eventually appear. Because it was inevitable, it was almost a relief.

Mitchell:

Please come by my office for a conference upon arrival. Thank you.

Mayfield

Will knew it was about Josh.

"For eight long, tedious, wasteful months, including many a Saturday and Sunday, you have attempted to get this man to relive his horrible experience," said Dr. Mayfield, always the professional in his white coat over a white shirt. "You have not only *not* helped him deal with his severe lunacy, I believe you have made it worse. Your theory, that reliving the experience in the extreme will help him recover from his lunacy, is absurd and you have proved it so."

"Maybe it takes more time," Will mumbled. In a burst of anger, he added, "Trying to help him is better than killing—"

"Help him?" Mayfield interrupted. "As a physician, Dr. Mitchell, you are, in fact, violating the first rule of our calling. You are doing harm."

Will could not argue that point. Yesterday, like most days now, just the sight of Will had thrown Josh into a screaming fit. The poor man still had yet to utter a regular normal word. Except when he was yelling, he remained mute. Will knew he was not qualified to help lunatics, and he had proved it beyond any doubt with Josh, a pathetically sick man.

Dr. Mayfield's large windowless office occupied a corner in the basement off the treatment and other infirmary rooms. It was painted pale green and outfitted in furniture that matched that used by the patients. The big desk and five or six chairs scattered around were all cheap, institutional. So were the bookcases and the coffee table where Will was now sitting, across from Mayfield. There were a couple of books and a folder on the table. Will was sure they related in some way to him and to Josh.

"I have asked you here this morning, Dr. Mitchell, to give you a lecture—not in any hostile or disciplinary way, however," said Dr. Mayfield. "I want you to learn from this experience. I want you to understand what you have done."

"As I said, I tried to help the man, that's all I've done," said Will. He was not interested in any kind of lecture.

"I would take you back a step, Dr. Mitchell. Do you believe you helped him in saving him from a beneficial death last year?"

"Yes. I am a physican committed to the premise that any life, even that of an incurable lunatic, is always worth saving."

"I would submit that, by *saving* him, you denied him the right to be useful." Dr. Mayfield picked up one of the books on the coffee table. It was dark brown, the same color as his tie, and about the thickness of a dictionary. "This contains a glimpse into what the future may hold for the treatment of lunacy. Some impressive research results are beginning to point to chemical imbalances in the brain as being a primary cause. That might mean a future that could involve merely prescribing medicines for the treatment of ailments such as the one that afflicts your man Lancaster. It's a future that must be realized as fast as possible. This institution and hundreds more like it are filling up and brimming over with the hopeless and the damned, in this country alone. We have no time to waste, Dr. Mitchell. We must work as fast as possible, using every means at our disposal. And that requires the use of expedited research on those diseased brains that—"

Will jumped to his feet. "Thank you for the lecture, Dr. Mayfield," he said. "I appreciate your sincerity and I'll admit I have been unable to help poor Josh—not in eight months, at least. But killing people, even in the name of expediting the treatment of lunatics, is murder under the laws of the state of Missouri and of God."

"You will have nothing more to do with Joshua Alan Lancaster unless it is to treat a physical ailment," Dr. Mayfield said. "Is that clear?"

It was clear. Will left the office.

He was tempted to gather up what few things he had in his room at the doctors' residence and get the hell out. Forget the rest of his two-year commitment. Forget this interesting experience. Move on to the practice of normal medicine on normal people in normal Kansas City, Missouri.

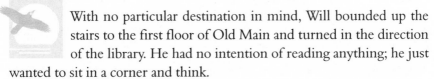

With no particular destination in mind, Will bounded up the stairs to the first floor of Old Main and turned in the direction of the library. He had no intention of reading anything; he just wanted to sit in a corner and think.

In looking for such a corner, he came across Josh. Joshua Alan Lancaster. His conversation with Mayfield was the first time Will had heard Josh referred to by his full name.

Josh was sitting at a table surrounded by books.

"Hey, Josh," he said.

Josh blanched. His whole body cringed.

"Relax, please," Will said quickly. "I'm not here to do anything to you. I was just passing through. May I sit down?"

Josh remained stolid, unmoving. At least he didn't scream. That's progress, thought Will, as he took a seat across the table.

He glanced at what Josh was reading. It was a little green pamphlet called *Thrilling Record* by a Sergeant Thomas M. Goodman. Down in the corner, Goodman was identified as "the only survivor of the Centralia (Missouri) Massacre, September 27, 1864." On the table next to it was *History of Centralia, Missouri* by Edgar Thomas Rodemyre. Also *Quantrill's War* by Duane Schultz, *They Called Him Bloody Bill* by Donald R. Hale, and *Bloody Bill Anderson* by Albert Castel and Thomas Goodrich. Every one of the five or six books laid out in front of Josh appeared to be about the same thing: the events in and around Centralia, Missouri, during the Civil War. All Will remembered from his high school history class was that these men were pro-Confederate guerrillas, called bushwhackers, who roamed the state committing unspeakable acts of violence against pro-Union people and their possessions.

Josh seemed to be using all the books at the same time. How could that be? And his lips were moving, even though no sound was coming from them.

Will decided to try to get Josh to talk one more time. Maybe there was something going on here with these books.

"What's the worst thing those bushwhackers did?" Will asked, figuring that getting an answer from a man who hadn't spoken a calm word in almost fifteen years was at least worth another try.

"They scalped some of the Union soldiers they murdered at Centralia,"

Josh said, in a direct, articulate, modulated performance voice. "Before Centralia, they cut off the noses and ears of their victims, too."

Will couldn't believe *his* ears. This patient on the other side of this table was speaking!

"Tell me more about what happened at Centralia," Will said, as calmly as he could, afraid to let too much excitement show in his voice.

Josh told him the story of the Centralia massacre in detail without referring to a note or a page from any book. It was a recitation, almost an act. He spoke as if there should be quotation marks around each of his sentences. He had clearly memorized passages from the books in front of him and strung them together to form a story with a beginning, a middle, and an end.

Will was astonished—stunned—at the accomplished way Josh recited the story, changing the tone and inflection of his voice to fit various characters.

"That was most impressive," Will said, when Josh finished. "You spoke just like a real actor would."

Josh smiled. "Well, to tell you the truth, doctor, all of it does come from these books, mostly word for word. I've done very little else except read these books ever since I got here. The words are pretty much a part of me now."

"Why? Why did you do this?"

"It was something to do, something to keep me occupied."

Will wondered if Josh realized what he had just that moment done. He had had a conversation! In addition to the memorized sentences, he had spoken real ones of his own. *Four* real ones.

"Congratulations, Josh. Congratulations, congratulations. You have broken your silence. Memorizing those words about Centralia broke your silence."

Will saw a look of wonder on Josh's face. He shook his head and gazed down at the books. "Yes!" he said in a whisper. "I'm talking!"

Will Mitchell, ordinary MD, was then struck with an idea that might help Josh even more. "Have you ever tried to think of the Centralia massacre as you went to sleep?"

Josh shook his head. "No," he said tightly.

"Maybe the only way to deal with your own massacre is to think about somebody else's. Give it a try, Josh. Close your eyes right now and think only of Centralia—from the beginning—just like you told it to me."

Josh, clearly skeptical and fearful, kept his eyes wide open for one second, two, three, four. . . .

Then he suddenly closed them.

He kept them shut for a minute . . . and another minute. . . . When he finally opened his eyes four minutes later, they were filled with tears of joy.

XII

JOSH AND BIRDIE

UNION STATION

1933

Birdie stretched his arms out as if they were wings.

"Make the sound of a crow for me, Josh," he said.

Josh tried. No noise came from his mouth, but he was pleased to see that Birdie was better—calmer. He seemed almost happy. Who knows what happened to him? thought Josh. Who knows anything about lunatics?

Birdie made his own crow music as he began a quick swooping circle around the small space at the rear of the train. He sounded more like a croaking frog or a neighing horse than a squawking crow. But it didn't seem to matter to him.

"Here we are," he said, as he stopped and lowered his arms. "Two flown crows, about to land at Union Station on The Flying Crow. No matter what happens, no matter who finds us, don't you feel like a flown crow right now, Josh?"

Josh said nothing. He had not spoken since they climbed onto the back of the train fifty minutes ago. He had sat, silent and motionless, on the platform in a corner against the open rear of the observation car. His senses took in the motion of the moving train and the blustering wind. He heard the *clickety-clack* of the wheels on the track and the loud blares of the whistle—two longs, a short, and a long—as the train passed over grade crossings and through tiny Missouri towns on the way to Kansas City. But he hadn't talked—or moved.

"Flown crows feel like they've been flying straight," Birdie yelled, answering his own question. "Here we are, Birdie and Josh, having just flown straight as the crow flies. Straight from the Somerset lunatic asylum to Union Station. That's us, flown crows."

Birdie could talk as loud as he wanted to now, as the train crept slowly into the main yards of Union Station. In a few moments, someone somewhere would throw a magic switch to direct it to a particular track for its arrival below the Union Station building.

Josh's original plan for Birdie was based on the probability that no conductor or any other person, passenger or employee, aboard The Flying Crow would have an occasion to check the outside observation deck at the rear of the train this time of morning, this close to its final destination. He had been right. They had made their stolen trip from Somerset to Kansas City undetected.

The train's brakes screeched.

"Hey, Josh, here we are!" Birdie said, his voice going higher and higher. "Up on your feet. Welcome to *the* Union Station!"

Josh did not move.

"I used to come here on Saturday mornings with my cousin Paul," Birdie said. "He was a paperboy for the *Star*—the *Kansas City Star*. On Saturdays I'd come with him and help him sell papers. I loved it. I love this place so much!"

Josh couldn't imagine loving a train station. Loving people was hard enough. But this was Birdie. He was some strange kid. He seemed scared to be coming here one minute, and now he was talking like a kid at the circus, at his favorite place.

"Come on, Josh, come on! We'll have to be careful, but let me show you around. Let me show you my Union Station, my massacre."

So Birdie really did see something awful at a train station?

When he got no response, Birdie came over to Josh and leaned down. "You're a free man, Josh, free as a bird, a crow, just like I am—thanks to you. No more rocking in those chairs, sweeping with those brooms, eating cheese sandwiches, running around naked, sitting in water for hours—and mostly no more ball bats to the head. Nothing could be worse than that; that's what I decided. Yeah, yeah, that's what I decided. Everything's going to be fine now."

Josh wanted to say something about who really decided what about leaving Somerset. And he wanted to say something else about some things being worse than living at Somerset—at least for him. Who knew about Birdie. But Josh couldn't speak or move. His body, his mind, and his mouth were frozen in place.

Josh trembled at the last long squeal of the brakes. The train stopped. He could hear the noise of people on the platform. The noise of regular people in the outside world was something he had not heard in years.

Birdie jerked his hat down farther on his head and turned up the collar on his shirt. His eyes and nose were about all of his face that could be seen.

Birdie could do whatever he wanted, but Josh figured there was no point in doing anything like trying to hide his own face. He had to go back to Somerset as quick as he could no matter what.

Birdie grabbed Josh by his shoulders and pulled him to his feet. Josh did not resist. "You took care of me at Somerset, Josh, and now I'm going to take care of you," Birdie said. "Think of me as your nephew. Or son. No, no, not any of those: friend. You are my friend. I am your friend. How old are you anyhow?"

Josh did not answer Birdie's question. Ages, like last names, were things that didn't matter at the Sunset in Somerset.

"You've got to be at least double my age, maybe triple—forty, sixty, one hundred, who knows? Who cares? We're friends, Josh."

Josh, still silent, accepted Birdie's arm around his shoulder and his help in climbing up and over the ornate fencing onto the station platform. If anybody in authority—a conductor, a porter, a cop—saw them leave the train, they must not have cared because nobody stopped them or said anything.

Birdie tucked his head even farther down into his body in an attempt, it seemed to Josh, to be invisible. Josh couldn't figure what Birdie was so scared of. Wasn't it too soon for anyone to have gotten the word from Somerset to be on the lookout for two escaped lunatics? Birdie didn't seem to think so.

They started walking forward with the train on their left like any other two arriving passengers.

"I love this place," said Birdie, keeping his head down, his voice soft. "I always loved coming here with Paul, being here—except for that awful morning. I didn't love that."

The jumble of noise and commotion on the platform was suddenly too much for Josh. It overwhelmed him and he stopped. Birdie grabbed him around the shoulders again and propelled him forward.

"It's OK, Josh. It's OK. Stick with me. I won't let anybody catch us, either of us."

Passengers were still getting off the train, scurrying ahead of Josh and Birdie toward some distant stairs. Men wearing red caps were calling for customers who needed help with their luggage. Men in dark blue uniforms with billed caps, starched white shirts, and black bow ties were hawking items from shops on wheels with signs over them that said TRAV-

ELERS' NEEDS. One sold magazines, cigarettes, apples, and candies; another offered hot coffee and slices of coffee cakes and cinnamon rolls.

"We're at Track Three, but it doesn't matter because they're all the same," Birdie said. "Track Twelve was where it started, where the train came in from Arkansas on the morning of my massacre."

Side by side, Josh and Birdie continued down the concrete platform, passing the first and then the second movable shop. They could hear the engine of The Flying Crow, its bell at the front still ringing, steam hissing out from underneath the wheels.

Words continued to tumble out of Birdie, but nobody except Josh could possibly have heard what he was saying—and Josh barely could.

"There's no *Star* boy here. Somebody's missing a big bet; somebody ought to be meeting this train with the *Kansas City Star.* Passengers on these early trains haven't had a chance yet to pick one up. Somebody ought to be here with the first paper they'll have had a chance to buy anywhere since they woke up on the train. Paul knew that. I'd come with him on Saturdays. Smart, huh, Josh?"

Josh nodded. None of what Birdie was saying made sense to him. Maybe this kid had a lot more mental problems than not being able to close his eyes without screaming. . . .

Birdie suddenly stopped and looked back toward the rear of the train. "I thought I saw a policeman back there. Did you see a policeman, Josh?" There was alarm in his voice.

Birdie motioned for Josh to look, too. There were only a few slow-moving passengers behind them, coming their way.

After letting out a long breath of relief and turning completely around to look in all directions, Birdie said, "I was down here that morning to meet the Missouri Pacific's Southerner, Josh. Most of the trains have names—you know, like people do, like The Flying Crow does. Burlington's are Zephyrs, the Rock Island's are Rockets. Did they do that with the trains when you were you—you know, before you went to Somerset?"

Josh couldn't remember. It wasn't something that stuck in his mind one way or another. This was the kind of crazy train talk Birdie should have had with Streamliner. Josh wondered about himself. Words wouldn't come. What had come over him? Was he having a relapse of some kind? He was afraid for himself. He had to get back to Somerset as fast as possible. Had fear locked up his ability to speak?

Again, Birdie went on without an answer. "Could be that telling you and showing you what happened to me here at Union Station makes me crazier. Can you stay with me and help me forever?"

Josh ached to speak but still couldn't. He wanted to say, Had you stayed any longer at Somerset you'd really be crazier—maybe even dead. Although you're looking and sounding crazier and crazier with each passing second now. But no matter how crazy you get, I can't stay with you. I have to return to Somerset.

"Hey, Josh," Birdie said, "don't think I haven't noticed you're not talking. I don't know what's come over you, but that's OK. Like I said a while ago, we're going to help each other."

Josh didn't want or need any help. Right now he just wanted to do what he could for Birdie and then get back to Somerset.

Birdie said, "You never did really return to your train station in Centralia the way I'm doing now, did you?"

Josh shook his head and then touched his temple with the index finger of his right hand.

"Got it, yeah, yeah, your thing on the stage in the auditorium. You went back in your mind. That must be quite a bloody story you tell. Sorry I never saw your big performance. My story's got some blood, too. Mostly from one guy in the car. . . ."

Birdie started to close his eyes and then suddenly opened them wide— as if remembering something. His body shook.

Josh patted Birdie on the back. But, still, no words would come.

After a couple of seconds, however, like a short breeze, whatever was happening to Birdie passed on. And his low babble continued.

"The Southerner was due in at seven-fifteen A.M., and the men in the stationmaster's office said it was going to be about fifteen minutes late. Think what that means. That train left New Orleans at something like ten o'clock at night on June fifteenth, 1933, went all night and day on June sixteenth up through Louisiana and Arkansas, and then went all night a second night before getting to Kansas City in the morning on June seventeenth only fifteen minutes late. They all did that, those Santa Fes. I love those big Santa Fes; they go to Chicago one way and to California the other and do the same thing—maybe more, maybe three nights, I think— before they get to one end or the other, Los Angeles or Chicago. Think about how hard that must be for the engineers and the brakemen and the other guys who work on the trains to get them to where they're finally going on time—or just fifteen minutes late. Threading a needle at night with no light and no fingers is what it's got to be like. Only fifteen minutes late, say at seven-thirty, like that Missouri Pacific did the morning of June seventeenth. That's something, isn't it, Josh?"

Josh nodded agreement. Why is Birdie going on and on like this? But, come to think of it, Josh couldn't even imagine having the ability to make a train arrive at a place exactly when it was supposed to, at the right time or even the right day. He knew there were people born into this world who could do such things but he wasn't one of them. He was an approximate man, not an exact man.

As they walked down the platform, Josh noticed that Birdie, most of his face still hidden by his hat and his collar, was keeping a constant nervous lookout. But he never stopped talking.

"I was running by the time I got right about here, because I could see and hear the Missouri Pacific train coming in. I remember thinking the stationmaster was wrong; it wasn't quite seven-thirty yet. But there it was. I stood right here as the engine went by, blowing steam and clanging its bell, and the fireman on the right side waved at me, and then came the baggage car and a chair car or two, and then came the sleeping cars. Those were the ones I was keen on because I figured they carried the passengers rich enough and interested enough in the news to buy a newspaper. Yeah, yeah. Smart, huh?"

Josh didn't respond. He so wanted Birdie to shut up. He knew telling his story was helpful to Birdie, but the noise of the telling was getting to be too much for Josh.

"The first sleeping car—there were two sleepers on that train—stopped right in front of me. I sure admire the way train engineers, not only on the Missouri Pacific but all of them, like the one on The Flying Crow just now, can stop those trains on a dime, right where they're supposed to be on the track.

"I could see a man, a passenger, leaning out from the first sleeping car like he was looking for somebody. He waved at a couple of men standing next to me. They were both in suits and hats. I hadn't noticed before, but they were both carrying pistols. One had his in his belt, the other in his right hand.

"People started coming from the rest of the train, and then I saw the waving man get off the train with four other men, all carrying guns, big ones—shotguns is what they looked like. The men were in suits and ties and felt hats and looked tough, like crooks or cops. Right behind them came a guy with his hands together in front of him, fastened by a pair of shiny silver handcuffs. Some more guys with guns got off the train next, and with the two men already waiting on the platform they formed a little V formation, with the guy in handcuffs in the middle down in the point of the V and the others with suits and guns fanning out a little forward on each side. I couldn't believe it. I knew—no, I knew nothing; I figured, I guessed—he was some crook and the cops were taking him somewhere, most likely to prison, but I was just guessing. You believe me, don't you, Josh?"

Josh nodded. Why would he not believe the kid? Why was he asking these questions?

"I found out later—along with everyone else in the world—that the guy was named Frank Nash: Jelly Nash, they called him. They said he had escaped from Leavenworth federal prison, just north of here up in Kansas, but he actually just walked out like he owned the place. They said—the papers said it and I read it later—that he had become a trustee in the warden's office by acting like he had turned over a new leaf from reading William Shakespeare books he got from the prison library—which he stole, by the way, when he escaped. *You* didn't steal any books because you didn't know you were escaping, did you, Josh?"

Josh wasn't sure how much more of this he could take. He wanted to help Birdie, but he really had to start figuring out how he was going to get himself back to Somerset. . . .

Birdie moved back to what happened to Jelly Nash. "They finally caught Nash in Hot Springs, Arkansas, and the cops and federal agents were taking him back to Leavenworth. They got on the Missouri Pacific's night train in Fort Smith, and they were going to drive him up to Leavenworth from the train here, right back to prison. That's what the paper said was their plan. I didn't know any of this at the time, of course. No way did I know any of that. Some people may not ever believe me, but that's the truth!"

Those words came out as if Birdie were pleading with somebody, not just telling a story. Josh didn't know what to think.

"All I knew was here was something pretty special coming right at me in V formation down the train platform. This was big, this was exciting. Coming right at me, walking toward me down a platform like this one, came a crook with his hands cuffed and cops with shotguns all around him. The other people scattered to both sides like pigeons, leaving a big hole for the men in the V to walk through."

Birdie grabbed something out of his coat pocket and put it up to his nose. It was pink, a woman's kerchief. "Sister Hilda gave this to me. I may look her up. She said she liked to stay with a sister who lived on Garfield beyond Troost, just off the Brooklyn Avenue streetcar line. I know exactly where that is."

Josh wanted to yell, You really are crazy! Fooling around with her already almost got you killed and it could again, and it could get her in even more trouble than she is probably in already. Leave the poor lady alone!

Birdie stuck the kerchief around his neck and tied it loosely. It covered up even more of what was left of his face to see.

Then he turned and started walking away from the tracks, and so did Josh. They were headed toward a flight of stairs marked with an overhead sign: TO STATION.

"My cousin Paul told me there are forty-four steps to climb up to the walkway that'll take us into the station," Birdie said.

Forty-four steps? Who in their right mind goes around counting the number of steps in a train station? thought Josh. Maybe Birdie's cousin was crazy too. He had heard that a lot of lunacy was inherited.

Birdie, not slowing his pace or moving his head, said to Josh, "Once we get upstairs in the station with all the people, don't look anybody in the eye. Keep your head down. There could be cops and maybe some other people strolling around looking for us. Just in case, keep walking like we're ordinary passengers just off The Flying Crow, two honest, simple, harmless flown crows. Don't look at anybody. Crows don't look at live people walking anyhow. They only pay attention to dead things in the middle of the road. Isn't that right, Josh?"

Josh didn't answer. He was really worried about Birdie.

The kid was walking almost in a crouch, trying to make himself even smaller, trying to act invisible. Josh wondered if ordinary people in a train station—not cops or doctors or bushwhackers—could pick out people who have just escaped from a lunatic asylum. Escaped: is that what we did? We just left on the train. Yes, we escaped. Is somebody already looking for us? Maybe, sure. Somebody could have told somebody who told somebody else who told the police here at the Kansas City Union Station that we were on The Flying Crow. Two escaped lunatics, one of them accused of having copulated with the wife of a bank vice president, are on The Flying Crow! Streamliner didn't see anything. Only Lawrence of Sedalia really knew what happened and he wouldn't tell anyone. Birdie aside, Lawrence's happiness over having Josh stop his Centralia performance would have kept him silent.

But that's not going to help us at this train station, thought Josh. Do lunatics look different from other people? That's the question. I'm tall, skinny, big-nosed, very white. My eyes are blue, my hands are huge, my hair is brown and long. Birdie looks like the black-haired kid that he is. Are we dressed OK? Most of the other men here are wearing suit coats and ties. Our blue shirts and pants say we could be construction workers. Is there something in our eyes that's different? Can they tell our heads have been hit by baseball bats and our bodies have been immersed for hours in tubs of water like hippopotamuses and we have rocked in chairs and pushed brooms for hour after hour after hour? They can see all of my face but only a tiny bit of Birdie's. . . .

Birdie said to Josh, "Ever wonder why the Kansas City Southern named their train The Flying Crow? Don't all crows fly? What's so special about that?"

Josh didn't know or care. He wanted to say to Birdie that he should have asked Streamliner about all that crazy stuff. Although, as far as Josh could tell, Streamliner didn't really have two-way conversations about The Flying Crow or any other thing.

They walked over to the stairway, the forty-four steps. Nobody else was around.

"We'll take it easy going up, old man—friend," Birdie said. "Do you want to get some bacon and eggs over easy with toast and grapefruit juice and coffee with sugar and fresh cream from the Adams dairy before we do anything—you know, outside with the massacre? The Fred Harvey House upstairs in the lobby has the greatest of everything there is to eat in Kansas City—in the world, probably. They even have a soda fountain and, next to it, a fancy restaurant with white tablecloths and silverware that weighs a ton. That's where the rich people come."

Josh shook his head.

"Forget it anyhow," Birdie said. "We haven't got any money. Unless we can find somebody who'll give us some money or some food, we're out of luck."

Their pace was slow, with Birdie stopping every four or five steps to glance around. It had nothing to do with Josh's health or age.

At the top of the forty-four stairs they entered what Birdie called the *midway,* a long corridor that he said led off to the right into the big station building itself.

Josh didn't know what to expect. He had never been inside a big train station, in Kansas City or anywhere else.

They entered the grand lobby through a door underneath a sign that said FROM TRAINS, took a few steps, and stopped.

What lay before them was the most spectacular sight ever to hit Josh's eyes. Was it a mirage, a picture in a travel book, a beautiful dream? There was a high ceiling that seemed to go way up in the sky, which was painted with red and cream and green and blue curlicues and symbols and designs and ornaments. Chandeliers hung higher than Josh had ever seen in a building. There were people everywhere, walking and running in all directions, and there were the deep, metallic voices of men on PA systems announcing trains, and men selling food and drinks and magazines and newspapers, and more men in red caps offering to carry people's suitcases.

To Josh, it seemed like a carnival, a circus, in the grandest, most elegant, and busiest place in the world.

He glanced about several times, trying to take it all in. They were standing in what was essentially the cross of a giant T-shaped building. Behind them was the main waiting room, going straight north, with the grand lobby going out from the southern end east and west.

There was the Harvey House and its restaurants that Birdie had mentioned and a drugstore on the left. A door marked WOMEN'S WAITING ROOM was farther on the left, on the north. And the ticket office, a large half circle, came out from the main south wall with little windows with brass bars, twenty or thirty of them.

Josh was so absorbed in looking around that he failed to notice that Birdie had stopped jabbering. His mouth wasn't moving but his eyes were sure darting around.

"Don't you just love this place, Josh?" Birdie said in a near whisper.

Josh started to answer, to finally talk. But he was too emotional at the moment to come up with the right words to express the overpowering affection and good feelings he had at this flashing, moving moment for the Union Station in Kansas City.

Birdie, still moving his eyes around, started babbling again.

"There's supposed to be a depression, but look at all these people running around here with smiles and good clothes on. Somebody told me that when this station opened they had two days of parades through downtown Kansas City, and governors came here, and the president of the United States sent a telegram. I think that was back around 1915, during the war against the Germans. They said a lot of our soldiers came through here later, on their way to the front. One of my uncles was in the army, but he didn't go any farther than Camp Funston, a place over at Fort Riley in Kansas. Can you imagine going to war to kill Germans at the front and only being sent over the state line to Kansas? Did you know about the World War, Josh?"

Josh just moved his head slightly. It was no real answer. A couple of shell-shocked patients came to Somerset afterward who had been made crazy by what they saw or did as soldiers in the war. Josh got to know a few, but most of them were eventually locked up in Beech with the incurables. One of them told Josh about watching his best friend, also an American soldier, go nuts one morning and stick the barrel of his rifle into the mouths and ears of five little French girls. He blew their heads to smithereens. But Josh never talked to him or anyone else about what the war was about or who was fighting and why.

With Birdie still leading the way, they turned left toward the main waiting room, walking through a large entranceway, and under a round clock, at least six feet in diameter, that hung from the ceiling. Josh looked up to check the time. It was eight-forty-nine in the morning. He had never before checked the time on such a gigantic and elegant timepiece.

The waiting room was another spectacular sight, with ceilings almost as high as those in the lobby. Right down the center there was a large aisle as wide as a highway separating two series of row after row of double-sided, dark-brown, high-backed wooden benches for passengers to sit on while waiting for their trains. There were hundreds of people there this morning. Some were reading newspapers or books, others were sipping coffee or biting into rolls or fooling with babies or talking among themselves or just sitting there, some with their eyes closed, others wide-eyed. Were they thinking about where they were going on the train and what they might do there?

On both the east and the west sides of the room there were tall doorways, each closed off by an ornate steel gate and above it a two-foot-high numeral. Even track numbers were on the right side, odd numbers on the left.

A couple of the gates were open and a man in uniform was looking at the tickets of people as they passed through to their trains. Long black destination signs hung on either side of the door that had in large white letters the name of the train and the towns it was going to. Josh stopped to read one of them.

9:30 A.M.
FRISCO R.R.
No. 117

THE FIREFLY

Ft. Scott
Miami
Tulsa
Oklahoma City
Pittsburg
Joplin

Josh felt a hard shove from behind. "There's a cop," said Birdie quietly. He had done the shoving. "Don't turn around. Look at the sign, look at the sign."

Josh had no choice but to keep his eyes on The Firefly's sign. A cop? Why was that a problem? But again he read the towns served by the Frisco train. He figured being found by a policeman might even be a relief. He would explain nicely that he had made a serious mistake in leaving the Somerset asylum; he was sorry and was ready to return. But it was different for Birdie. He wasn't going back to Somerset. He couldn't go back without risking his life. . . .

After at least a minute, Birdie whispered, "Let's go."

They headed back toward the grand lobby and stopped under the big clock. There were people everywhere, none of them, it seemed to Josh, the least bit interested in him or Birdie.

Birdie looked up at the clock. "I was still with the crook and the cops—behind them, right behind them," Birdie said, picking up his story. He seemed more relaxed. Had the policeman seen his face and done nothing about it? Maybe that meant nobody was looking for them yet. Josh had no idea.

"I wasn't going to miss a second of this, whatever was going on. If I had known what was going to happen I wouldn't have minded missing it, that's for sure. It made me crazy. I still am crazy, Josh. You have to stay with me and help me live a normal life."

Birdie led them diagonally and quickly across the left front of the ticket office, past the newsstand and a small Travelers Aid booth, toward the main doors on the east side of the ticket office. There was a matching set of doors on the west side.

"There were crowds that morning just like now. Most of them saw the V formation and the guns. They moved out of the way, but they wanted to see what was happening. I could see everything. It was really like a movie."

Birdie pointed to the Travelers Aid booth. A young black-haired woman in a red dress was behind the counter. "There was supposed to be a different, older lady there that morning, but I didn't see her. Later she said she saw the whole massacre, but I don't think she did because she wasn't anywhere around until after the shooting started. There were a lot of people who *said* they saw things that I don't think they really saw."

Birdie suddenly realized that in telling his story he had allowed his face to become exposed, so he adjusted his hat and collar and kerchief to cover himself more.

They were at the big doors that led outside, seven or eight of them, each at least ten feet tall, glass framed in heavy bronze. Josh had seen pictures of doors like these in books but never in person.

Birdie pushed open a door in the middle and Josh followed him outside. "I was still right with them . . . behind them."

He stopped on the sidewalk barely three yards from the door, still under a canopy that protected passengers from the entranceway out to the curb and the roadway for taxis and drop-offs in front of the station.

"This is as far as I should have gone that morning, I guess," Birdie said. "I don't know what made me keep walking, moving with the cops and the crook. I knew . . . I could see where they were headed. There was a row of cars parked there, just like now."

Birdie stepped off the curb onto the roadway. He pointed straight ahead another ten yards to a line of cars, parked head-on against a curb facing south, away from the station.

"The cops in front opened all the doors on one car—"

Birdie suddenly threw his hands up to his eyes and spun around, back toward the station. "No! The blood! Don't shoot no more!"

Josh grabbed Birdie and held him close until the screaming stopped. It was only to a count of five or six.

"You see, Josh, you see? I'm still crazy. It didn't work. I still need your help. See?"

Josh guided Birdie back into the station, weaving through the people, passing at an angle between the Travelers Aid booth and the ticket windows, across the grand lobby, and under the clock into the waiting room.

They walked down the center aisle to the very end of the room, turning only after reaching the last row of benches, at the waiting area for Track 16. There were no people there. Josh set Birdie down on the dark wooden bench.

"You OK, Birdie?" Josh asked.

Birdie smiled and straightened. "Thanks for talking again, Josh," he said, almost as if nothing had just happened. "I was beginning to worry about you more than me."

There's nothing I've been doing that's half as crazy as what you've been up to, Josh thought, but he did not say it. Instead, he said to Birdie, "Stay right here. I'm going to be gone for a few minutes."

Josh knew he had to go back to Somerset. But he just could not leave Birdie here at the train station in this condition. Only one person might be able to help.

 The woman in the red dress at the Travelers Aid desk flashed a sympathetic smile from the very beginning of Josh's request for assistance.

"My friend is ill and I need to talk to his doctor," Josh said, trying not to sound to this woman like somebody who might have just escaped from a lunatic asylum.

"It doesn't surprise me that he's sick. I couldn't help noticing the two of you passing by just now," said the woman, who Josh figured to be about thirty. "He was shaking so and his face was all covered up like he was feverish."

The woman reached under the counter and came up with a loose-leaf binder. "We have doctors on a special list to call—"

Josh held up his hand. "There's one doctor in particular who knows about his condition. He's a specialist. His name is Mitchell, Will Mitchell. Would you mind calling him and then letting me talk to him on the phone?"

Josh had no idea if Will Mitchell was still a doctor in Kansas City—or, for that matter, if he ever was. All he knew was that's what Will said he was going to do when he left Somerset in anger some thirteen years ago.

The woman shook her head slightly—officiously. "That's not how we do it, sir. The procedure is for us to summon one of the doctors who have been certified for volunteering to treat passengers here at Union Station. Otherwise, for an emergency or anything else, we're to get the Kansas City Police officer on duty to see whether an ambulance is necessary."

"If you could, just this once, make an exception. His name is Mitchell. Dr. Will Mitchell."

She looked down at her list of doctors.

"His name's not here. He's not a certified volunteer."

"Could you look him up in the phone book possibly? I would be forever grateful, I really would."

"What's wrong with your friend? What's his ailment?"

All right, here we are. A moment of a truth—that must be handled with a creative untruth.

"He's what the doctors call a crow maniac," Josh said. "He thinks he's a flying crow—you know, like the train from Texas, only a real one."

The young woman quickly grabbed another book from under the counter. In a matter of seconds, she said, "There is no Dr. Will Mitchell. There's a plain Dr. William Mitchell—no middle initial at all—a Dr. William A. Mitchell, and a Dr. William B. Mitchell."

Eagerly she went to work, setting down a black phone with a long cord between her and Josh. First, she dialed the four-digit number of the first William and said to someone exactly what Josh suggested that she say. "This is Wanda Levenger at Travelers Aid at Union Station. I'm telephoning for Dr. Mitchell on behalf of Josh of the Sunset at Somerset. Would the doctor have a few moments to discuss crows in Centralia?"

The third and last Dr. Mitchell was the right one.

"Josh, is that you?" Josh remembered that deep, happy voice as that of the man who had changed his life.

Wanda Levenger, clearly a person of tact and quality, on her own moved away from Josh so as not to be in a position to overhear his conversation.

"Yes, doctor, it's me," Josh said.

"What are you doing on a telephone? Where are you?"

"At Union Station."

"Where? What Union Station?"

"This one. Yours. The one in Kansas City. I came up here today from Somerset on the train, The Flying Crow."

"What? How did they ever let you go?"

"They didn't. I just left."

"What? You escaped?"

"You might say that. But it's complicated and it's medical. It was to help another man—quite a bit like me—who is here and needs your help. I've got to go back but I can't leave him yet."

"Where at the station are you?"

"In the big waiting room . . . the last row from the main entrance."

"I'll be right there, Josh."

It wasn't very long before Dr. Will Mitchell was indeed right there.

He and Josh shook hands and then grabbed each other's elbows and then, finally, embraced like brothers—friends.

"Damn, Josh, I don't have to tell you what kind of jeopardy you're placing yourself in. Unless something's changed about your case, if they think you're sane enough—"

"Meet Birdie," Josh said, not letting Dr. Mitchell finish his sentence. Josh knew all about his case and his jeopardy. There was no reason for Birdie to know too. This was about Birdie, anyhow.

Josh really did worship Will Mitchell, this special man in a dark blue suit and white shirt and pink tie now shaking hands with Birdie. Did he love him too? Josh knew the word and used the word but he had no idea what it really meant when it came to anybody, particularly somebody like Will Mitchell.

It had been nearly fourteen years since Josh had seen Will Mitchell. How old must he be now? At least forty, maybe forty-five. He seemed like just a kid when he was a doctor at Somerset. The hair was still curly, full and mostly red, though tinted now with some gray. The face was as bright white and smooth and open as ever. He had gained some weight, most of it having gone right to his stomach, a hunk of which hung down over his belt in clear view through his unbuttoned suit coat.

"This is the man who saved my life, and now he's going to save yours," Josh said to Birdie.

Will Mitchell's face didn't change expression. As Josh recalled, it seldom did, always maintaining a great combination of comfort and wonder. There was no way to look at the man and not feel at ease. There had even been the hint of a child in the way he listened to the stories and concerns and delusions of Josh and the other patients at Somerset.

Now, sitting on a bench at Track 16 between Josh and Birdie, he was listening again.

Josh did most of the talking at first, explaining Birdie's problem in closing his eyes without seeing the horror of what happened right here at this train station just a few months ago.

"That was some awful mess, I'm sure," Will Mitchell said to Birdie, in a tone that seemed to Josh to be a bit skeptical, like maybe he didn't believe Birdie's story. "My office is only a short distance from here. I heard the sirens that day and listened to everything I could on the radio. Some of the people in my office even drove over here to gawk like they were on some kind of sightseeing trip."

Birdie said there were a lot of people who did that. The parking lot out front was filled with gawkers within minutes after the killings.

"Did you see Pretty Boy Floyd?" Will Mitchell asked.

"I can't talk about that," Birdie said, with an edge of irritation. "I don't want you to tell anybody about any of this, either. Don't let anybody know you saw me here, now, in Kansas City or about me seeing the massacre. Do you promise as a doctor?"

Josh had not seen Birdie that way before.

Will Mitchell smiled, put his right hand over his heart, and said, "I do so promise."

Josh moved on quickly to tell Dr. Mitchell what had happened with

Birdie outside the station a short time ago as he tried to re-create the murder scene.

"Come with him now and help him finish it," Josh said. "It might really help him. He's been acting even more crazy since we got here."

Will Mitchell, the good and happy doctor, said no. "I'm not in that part of medicine, Josh. I closed out my life and times with massacres, lunacy, and the insane the day I left Somerset. That's over. A redcap at this train station would be as much help—professionally—as I would. I'm just a regular doctor. I listen to heartbeats, take pulses, set broken arms, and remove tonsils. In fact, I'm due to remove a twelve-year-old girl's tonsils in just over an hour. I'm sorry."

"It worked for me, why not for Birdie?" Josh said.

"That was all hunch and luck, Josh," Will said. "I didn't know what I was doing and I still don't. It was all dumb luck and maybe quackery—something I probably deserved to lose my license for."

Josh stood up and went into performance mode. Lowering his voice and looking straight over and past Will Mitchell as if he weren't there, he said, "I have to say now, dear listener, as I approach a description of the final horrors of the massacre, my voice grows weak, my sight is dimmed, and my heart sickens with the recollection. But I feel I have no choice, no alternative to completing this tale of terror and horror. Therefore, I must return to the details, sickening and atrocious as they are. . . ."

"You still do your act?" Will said, the childish expression dominating his face at the moment.

"I do indeed, on special occasions, for the entertainment of one and all," Josh said.

"I never saw it but I hear he's great," Birdie said.

"If it wasn't for you I wouldn't be doing it, and there's no telling what might have happened to me," Josh said to Will Mitchell.

The doctor dropped his head. "That's true, I guess," he said finally. "All right, let's give it a whirl. It doesn't make sense, but who am I to say?"

Walking three across with Birdie in the middle, they made their way out of the waiting room. Birdie kept his head way down inside his clothes. Josh gave a big wave and a wink to the Travelers Aid woman as they passed.

Everything's going to be just fine was his message to her.

They went through the big doors, still walking three abreast.

Dr. Mitchell stopped them outside after only a couple of steps. "All right, Birdie, what did you see?"

"Well, like I was telling Josh, I went with the cops and the crook—that Jelly Nash guy—out to the curb. They were going toward some cars parked just over there, facing away from the station, toward the south."

He didn't move. Neither did Dr. Mitchell or Josh. "I was watching them and I kept up with them, stepping off just in front of them—"

"I thought you were behind them," Josh said.

"Right, that's what I meant. I was behind them." Birdie laughed. It was a quick, unreal laugh, it seemed to Josh. There was nothing funny about any of this.

They moved together onto the road. Birdie's hands started shaking. Dr. Mitchell grabbed his right hand in his. "Go ahead, Birdie. Go ahead. What did you see?"

"They opened the doors of a car—"

Just as he had with Josh a short time ago, Birdie threw his shaking hands up to his eyes. Will Mitchell grabbed them and pulled them back down. "What happened next, Birdie?" he said. "Tell me what happened next."

"No, no. I can't."

"Who got in the car first? Just tell me that."

"It was Jelly Nash, the crook. They put him in through the door on the right, on the passenger side up front. He scooted across behind the steering wheel."

Will Mitchell was fighting to hold Birdie's hands down. "What were you thinking at the time, Birdie? What was going through your mind?"

"I thought, What's that all about? Why would they put the handcuffed guy in the driver's seat?"

"That was an understandable thought. Good."

"Yeah, but in a second or two I saw why. They did it so some of the guys with the guns—the cops—could get in back. It was a two-door sedan. They had to push up the front right-hand seat back so they could get in."

Josh gave Birdie a soft pat on the back. "You're doing great," he said.

Birdie glanced around to see that nobody was paying any attention to them and went on. "A couple of them climbed in the back, and then I saw two other men with guns coming at the car from the front. The guns were being carried with two hands. One of them looked like a submachine gun, you know, a tommy gun. The men were dressed like the others, in hats and coats and ties, but they were pointing the guns at the car and the cops. Another man came at them from the right and went almost right by me, paying me no mind—"

Birdie stopped suddenly.

Josh grabbed Birdie around the shoulders and pulled him into a hug as Birdie had done to Josh when they first got off The Flying Crow. "Keep talking, Birdie," Josh said. "I know it's hard for you, but I want to hear the whole story now. So does Dr. Mitchell."

Birdie shrugged and continued. "One of the gunmen yelled, 'Put 'em up! Up! Up!' There was a bang from the car, and then another. It was an explosion—louder than anything I had ever heard. Then came another. Just like that, almost at the same time."

Josh lowered his arm and let go of his grip on Birdie's shoulders.

"The car's windshield glass shattered. Jelly Nash's head blew to bits right there in front of me. His head was in pieces of skin, blood was spewing out of him, his hair went flying away. Later, I read it was a wig. I didn't know it then."

Will Mitchell released his hold on Birdie's hands.

"There were pops and flashes coming from the cops and the other guys with guns. I felt the wind from a bullet that went by me toward the station. Two of the cops fell right by the car, one on top of the other. Blood came gushing out of them. Everyplace I looked there was blood."

Birdie looked back toward the station. He took a deep breath and then let it out. Then he grinned—first at Josh, on his right, and then at Will Mitchell, on his left.

"Suddenly, like a switch had been pulled, it was over. There was shouting coming from behind me and the station. A cop came out of the station shooting a pistol and yelling. I looked around and saw redcaps and taxi drivers and passengers lying flat on the sidewalk.

"Then the gunmen ran back south, away from the blood and the cars and the cops and Jelly Nash. I couldn't tell where they went.

"The next thing I knew there were people everywhere, looking at the bodies and the car, yelling and screaming, and then there was the sound of sirens . . . and I was still standing there in the roadway, like a statue, like my feet were stuck to the pavement with cement."

Birdie fell silent. He looked down at his hands, which were still steady.

And he turned to face Josh. "I did it, Josh, I did it!" Birdie said. "I told the whole story, and I'm fine."

"That's right," Josh said. "Congratulations."

Will Mitchell put an arm around each man, Josh and Birdie, the two lunatics.

An impatient taxi driver was honking his horn for them to get out of the way. He clearly had a passenger who had come to Union Station to catch a train.

"If he only knew what a glorious achievement had just been accomplished in the middle of this road," said Dr. Mitchell, as the three of them moved onto the sidewalk, "he would be cheering and applauding."

He laughed. So did Josh and Birdie as they walked, three abreast, back toward the station.

"But maybe not," Birdie said, stopping.

"What do you mean?" Will Mitchell asked.

"Closing my eyes," Birdie said. Then he asked quickly, "Do you have any money?" They had taken only a couple of steps back inside the station.

Will smiled and said, sure, he had a few dollars on him.

Birdie, talking fast, said, "Josh here is starving. He told me he wanted some bacon and eggs over easy with toast, jam, and butter, plus a glass of grapefruit juice and coffee with heavy cream. How about treating Josh and me to some breakfast over there at the Harvey House?"

Will Mitchell shrugged an OK.

"We need to go somewhere like that where nobody can see us," Birdie added, scrunching up again.

Why would nobody see us in that restaurant called the Harvey House? thought Josh. The kid clearly still had some problems.

 Josh lowered his head, folded his hands behind his back, and began pacing in a circle around the stage. The idea was that he was thinking, pondering, considering.

He made two, three, and finally four complete circles before returning to center stage and stopping.

"I have to say now, as I prepare to repeat to you the last details of the mas-

sacre, that my spirit, my very being weakens at the prospect of my having to, once agan, relive those horrible moments. But I feel I have no choice, no alternative to completing this tale of terror and horror."

Josh sighed, took a deep breath, and then released it.

Speaking in soft voice, he finished the story.

"Anderson faced the line of soldiers. He said federal soldiers had scalped some of his men and left their bodies to rot on the ground.

" 'I am too honorable a man to permit any man to be scalped, but I will show you that I can kill men with as much skill and rapidity as anybody.' " he said.

"Again, the naked soldiers of the U.S. Army screamed for their lives, some even claiming they couldn't have had anything to do with scalping Anderson's people because they were off fighting in another part of the war. One poor doomed soul yelled that he had just come from being with Sherman in Georgia.

"Anderson responded with the final death sentence. 'I treat you all as one. You are federals and federals scalped my men and carry their scalps at their saddlebows.'

"I could not believe my no-longer-tender ears. Here was a man who had scalps of Union soldiers tied to his own saddle, acting as if it were only the other side who committed such atrocities. What a liar! What a barbarian! What an evil presence in this world!

"He then cocked his two revolvers. So did the other bushwhackers. I saw several of the soldiers turn their heads, their bodies, and close their eyes, waiting for the hot lead to pierce them.

"The bushwhackers fired. The terrific crashing sound shook the ground and my soul. I raised my hands to my ears to keep it away from me, but, alas, it was hopeless. The bushwhackers yelled like crazed maniacs; the soldiers cried. And within a few seconds, it was over. All but a few of the soldiers were dead or soon would be, bright red blood pouring from rough holes torn in their white skin. I saw one and then another still staggering around but soon they were downed by more bullets.

"Only one remained standing for long. His giant, naked body streaming blood, he rushed toward the bushwhacker executioners, knocked down several with his hands, then crawled under the train and disappeared beneath the station platform on the other side.

"Several bushwhackers went after him, then waited for the fire that was destroying the depot to do their dirty work. In only a few moments, the big man ran from the rear of the station, swinging a big piece of wood. He charged his attackers, knocking down two of them. But the others kept firing. He was hit time after time until he fell.

" 'My Lord!' he yelled from the ground.

"Then he was motionless. A bushwhacker put a bullet into the man's brain to make absolutely sure he never moved again.

"They did that to several of the soldiers on the other side of tracks too, silencing what few moans and other signs of vanishing life were still coming from their mouths.

"I watched with unspeakable horror as two of Anderson's barbarians showed him to be a full liar in front of everyone by whacking off the scalps of two dead soldiers. I turned my head from the scene at the very last few seconds, so thanks be to the Lord in heaven, I am unable to recount the exact sight of the two bushwhackers' knives removing the tops of the heads and I kept my eyes from drifting toward the scalpless heads afterward.

"It was then, and only then, that I ran away from this unspeakable sight as fast and as far as I could. Where was I when I stopped? Where was I? I have no recollection and I refuse to tax my mind to the point that I ever will. If I had had my wish, I would have been in a place so far away that I would be unable ever to recall where I had been and what I had seen.

"But, as you have just borne witness, that was not possible. I recall it now, and I will recall it forevermore."

Josh bowed deeply to the audience.

And then, in keeping with established and expected practice, there was chaos. Led by Lawrence of Sedalia, many of the patients started crying or screaming, some hid under chairs, some banged their heads against chairs or walls or one another, some stood on chairs with their hands and voices pleading upward for mercy to someone or something up there and away from here.

Josh continued to bow as if the uproar and noise were a form of applause for his performance.

All persons present seemed in a state of deep disturbance except the bushwhackers. In their dirty whites and with their Somerset Sluggers, they stood in the back and on the sides, watching and laughing at the collective misery of the others. To these present-day bushwhackers his story of the earlier bushwhackers seemed as entertaining as a radio show or a burlesque movie.

Yes, yes, Josh knew that was the point of the evening, the point of why *they let him do what he did. But he couldn't worry about that. Not now, not in these moments, when the sweet satisfaction of the performance was at its exquisite peak.*

He enjoyed being onstage, performing his lines perfectly, as he had tonight, exercising his truly extraordinary power to make people laugh and scream and be scared half out of their wits.

It didn't matter to him that his audience was made up of lunatics and bushwhackers.

XIII

RANDY

KANSAS CITY

1997

The file on Joshua Alan Lancaster arrived at the office in the regular mail. Randy had received no forewarning, no heads-up call from Simmons, the state police sergeant in Jefferson City, or anyone in Baxter County. The terrible story of Birdie Carlucci's best friend, Josh, simply arrived.

There were several pieces of paper in the 8-by-10 manila envelope. On top, attached by a paper clip, was a handwritten note on a sheet of white memo paper that had THE COUNTY OF BAXTER—OFFICE OF THE DISTRICT CLERK printed across the top.

Lieutenant Benton:

Rob Simmons asked that I retrieve and pass on this information. It took a while because the records are so old they were in a box in a corner of our courthouse not even the mice have visited in years. These are photocopies of the originals, which must remain in our files. If you need anything else, please feel free to contact me directly. Meanwhile, you owe me one. Rob too. That's what he told me to tell you.

Sincerely,
Diane Sams

Randy removed the note and the clip and began reading.

The first item was the handwritten report of a local law enforcement officer. It was dated June 25, 1905, Jensen City, Missouri.

I was in church this date, worshiping my Lord and Savior, when a young man of my acquaintance rushed into our sanctuary. "Marshal! Marshal Lloyd!" he screamed. "Come with me! There's been a massacre at the Lancaster farm!" I left the church with the young man, mounted my horse, and rode with him to the Lancaster farm, two and one half miles west on the Joplin road. I knew it to be the home of Wesley and Annie Lancaster, working farmers, loving parents, and good citizens of our community and state.

We arrived to find a boy of 15 sitting on the front porch. I recognized the lad as being Josh Lancaster, the eldest of three sons of Wesley and Annie. I knew them also to have a daughter. Josh was sobbing into his hands, which were covered with a red I knew was blood, as was his shirt, which had an original color of white, and trousers, which were dark blue. "I am so sorry. I don't know what happened. It's my fault. I am so sorry." Those expressions and similar ones were uttered repeatedly as I approached him and after I arrived at his side. I asked him what happened. He said he had killed his family. I asked him where his family was and he said, "In heaven, God willing." I said, "Yes, son, but where are they physically at this moment?" He pointed toward the front door of the house, which was wide open.

I entered a home that had become a place of horror and death beyond anything I had ever seen before, even in connection with my official duties. In the sitting room, there were the bleeding bodies of three children, known to me as the three other Lancaster children: Wesley Jr., 12, Charlotte, 10, and Lincoln, 8. Each had three or more sets of punctures in their stomachs and chests. In the kitchen was the body of Annie Lancaster, 37, similarly mutilated. Then, in a back bedroom, I came to the body of Wes Lancaster, 41. There were eight or nine sets of punctures across the front of his body, including his face. From the center of the stomach, there protruded the long wooden handle of a pitchfork. The prongs of the pitchfork remained deeply and fully embedded in the body of Wes Lancaster. My close examination of the pitchfork handle showed the presence of fingerprints in the blood that, to my trained and experienced eye, were not inconsistent with those of a young person.

I went through some quick actions, repulsive and upsetting to me in their execution, to ascertain that all five of the Lancasters were, in fact, deceased. I then returned to the porch. Josh Lancaster had not moved and had not stopped sobbing and, through words, was confessing and repenting for the horrible crimes he had just committed. His confession was not inconsistent with the fingerprint and other evidence that I observed and noted. As other citizens began arriving on the property, I asked Josh why he had done what he did. It took several askings, but finally he said only that his father had deprived him of an opportunity to love. He said nothing more that resembled coherence. I placed him under custody and transported him to the Baxter County jail in Jensen City. I did so after sending for Dr. Michael Adams to make the deaths official, for mortician Ben Quinn to remove and prepare the victims' physical remains for service and final resting, and for Pastor Willingham to prepare their souls for their departure to a Better Place. I gave custody of the bloody pitchfork, after it was removed from the body of Wes Lancaster, to county attorney Rick Smith.

William S. Lloyd,
City Marshal

Randy stopped reading, blinked his eyes, and took a deep breath. He could certainly see why Josh Lancaster chose to be a false witness to somebody else's massacre in Centralia rather than his very own.

There was more to the horrible story.

The next page, also handwritten, was the report of the doctor. Randy read it quickly. The doctor confirmed the five Lancasters were, in fact, dead. In each case, the cause of death was multiple and repeated punctures to their vital organs by an instrument believed to have been the sharp spokes of a pitchfork.

Then came the one-page charge—labeled a bill of indictment—against Joshua Alan Lancaster for the murders of his mother, father, two brothers, and sister. Attached to it was a legal-looking document signed by the county attorney recommending "with vigor and conviction" that despite the defendant's minor status he be put to death by hanging.

Below that paper was another signed by an attorney "on behalf of Joshua Alan Lancaster, minor."

It said:

There is God's evidence as well as that from ordinary mortals that proves beyond any doubt that Joshua Alan Lancaster was in a severe state of lunacy when he committed the heinous crimes for which he is charged and which he willingly and openly admits to having committed. Can anyone challenge the simple and direct premise that God would not have permitted a sane person to have committed such horrors? Only a person of a mind unsound beyond all medical or spiritual imagination could have done so. When coupled with the fact that the perpetrator is a mere lad of fifteen, the obviousness of the state of insanity becomes an even more overwhelming and unassailable truth. Why did he do it? He says to his lawyer and to the world that his father forbade him to take a certain young girl of our community to a festive occasion. Could that be reason for a person of sound mind to brutally destroy the lives of his entire family? Nay, I say! Nay, say the laws of God and of Missouri!

I, therefore, before the knowing God of us all and the merciful laws of our state of Missouri, beg the court to declare Joshua Alan Lancaster to have been insane beyond the ability to know what he was doing at the time he committed these horrible crimes. I plead for his life to be spared and for his sick, depraved mind to be treated.

Respectfully submitted,
Jonathan Lucas MacNair, Esq.

Then followed four pages of a transcript of a judicial proceeding a few weeks later.

The town marshal, William S. Lloyd, testified under oath that Joshua Alan Lancaster, a prisoner in the local jail, had been unable to close his eyes and sleep since the Sunday of the murders. He said the lad screamed "loud enough for God in heaven to hear and comprehend" each time his eyelids came shut. Attempts to induce sleep artificially had mostly been unsuccessful. On more than one occasion, said the marshal, he had resorted to knocking the boy out cold with carefully managed blows to the head. He said it was his opinion, as an officer of the law, that Joshua Alan Lancaster was "alive with the demons of what he had done" and the "sight of the horror he had created" came to focus each time he closed his eyes.

Dr. Michael Adams, the Jensen City physician, gave essentially the same testimony from a medical point of view. He said that putting Joshua Alan Lancaster to sleep or stopping him from screaming was beyond his expertise.

The last document in the packet was a copy of the final order issued by Judge R. Edward Keller.

Wrote the judge:

I find the defendant, Joshua Alan Lancaster, a minor at age fifteen, to be of unsound mind. I declare that he is a lunatic and certifiably insane under any standard the forces of our community and state could bring to bear on the question. I further find that he was of that condition shortly after twelve noon on June 25, 1905, when he wantonly and savagely ended the lives of his father, Wesley Richard Lancaster; his mother, Anne Lee (Richards) Lancaster; and his three minor siblings—Wesley Jr., Charlotte, and Lincoln.

I am mindful of the pleas from our esteemed county attorney that the nature of Joshua Alan Lancaster's crimes are such that the maximum penalty be imposed. I too have considered the competing pleas from counsel that his life be spared. The laws of our state, as currently enacted or litigated, give little definitive guidance in such a case. But in my reading I sensed a wide degree of latitude available to me in reaching a judgment. I have decided to exercise that latitude.

I therefore rule and order as follows: that Joshua Alan Lancaster be taken forthwith to the state lunatic asylum at Somerset. He shall remain there for the rest of his life without opportunity for parole or release. If at any time before his natural death it is determined that he is free of his lunacy, he should be taken into custody by the penal authorities of our state and put to death by hanging for the crimes he has committed.

So ordered this twenty-seventh day of August, 1905.

The Honorable R. Edward Keller

So. Here I am, thought Randy. One down, one to go. Now I know the full and terrible story of Joshua Alan Lancaster, but I'm still almost nowhere on Birdie Carlucci.

XIV

JOSH AND BIRDIE

UNION STATION

1933

After a glance around the restaurant, Birdie turned his attention to the Harvey Girls—the waitresses.

"Look at that splendid one over there, she's spotted me already, I'm sure," he whispered to Josh, pointing to a woman on the right side in the far rear of the restaurant. She was standing with her hands behind her back, looking at Birdie, Josh, and Will with a welcoming smile. "Let's do her the favor of sitting at one of her tables, what do you say? They're back in a corner, private-like."

Josh had never seen—or imagined—waitresses dressed like these. At a glance, they could pass for nuns. They had white collars around their necks and black bow ties at their throats, and they were covered down to their black shoes in huge white apron bibs over black long-sleeved blouses and white skirts. Everything about them seemed starched, including their hair, which was tucked neatly under hairnets. Unlike those at Somerset, thought Josh, here were some ladies who really should have *Sister* before their names.

There were at least ten of these young women moving around or waiting at particular tables throughout the restaurant, which appeared to be about half full of customers. They seemed most at home here because this Harvey House lunchroom had an extraordinary cathedral-like look and feel about it. The ceiling was two stories high; the white plaster walls were framed every several feet by intricate molding and decorated with lighting fixtures, each of which had three large ornate bulbs. In the center of the room was a long U-shaped counter with a marble top and swivel chairs that had caned backs and seats. Tables, also marble-topped, were arranged around it and also in a balcony in the rear that was not unlike a church choir loft.

And everywhere there were the fragrances of breakfast: frying eggs, sausage and bacon, syrup, strawberries, waffles, melted butter, coffee, hot cocoa, warm cinnamon rolls. . . .

Josh had never even imagined that an elegant place like this existed to prepare and serve food to people—especially to people like him. He hoped Will Mitchell had enough money to pay for what they ate.

"Good morning, and welcome to the Harvey House," said Birdie's well-chosen Harvey Girl. Under all that starch, Josh could tell there was a magnificent-looking brown-haired woman. She was very young, probably not more than eighteen or nineteen. Her blue eyes and her smile and her teeth gleamed, as did most everything else about her.

"What do your friends call you?" Birdie asked her, as he and Josh and Will sat down at a square table set with heavy silverware and folded white cloth napkins. Josh was awed by the preciseness of the way everything, including the salt and pepper shakers, was laid out. He was also hoping that Birdie behaved himself. This woman probably had a boyfriend—maybe even a husband—who would defend her honor with something equivalent to a Somerset Slugger.

"Janice," she said, giving each man a menu. "Even people who have just met me call me Janice."

Josh didn't think she addressed that remark in any special, alluring way to Birdie, but it was clear from the excited look on his face that Birdie took it that way. As with Sister Hilda, Birdie's very being was lunging toward this Harvey Girl named Janice.

"Janice is the single most beautiful name I have ever heard," said Birdie. "You are most properly named."

"Thank you," she said, as if it were something she was told several times a day. "I assume you are traveling men. Where are you traveling to or from today?"

"We came in on The Flying Crow—" Josh began.

Birdie interrupted. "No, no. We just happened in today from California on the Atchison, Topeka and Santa Fe," he lied. "We were out there looking for gold."

"Well, I certainly hope you found a lot," said Janice, looking more at Will than at either Birdie or Josh. Will was the one in a coat and tie. She had a small notebook and pencil ready to take their orders.

Birdie went first, choosing the bacon and eggs and toast and all the other things he had mentioned before. Josh, still adjusting to the situation, was unable to order at first. He also couldn't see the menu clearly because he had not brought his magnifying glass. But finally, through the blur, he did see a word that seemed to look like *pancakes,* so he ordered some of those and a glass of orange juice. Will had only a cup of coffee, explaining that he had already had breakfast at home before going to the office this morning.

While Janice went away to place their order and Birdie concentrated on watching her do so, Josh filled Will in on the latest news from Somerset: what doctors and bushwhackers were still around and which two new techniques were being tried on the patients. Will said he had read about both of them in medical journals; one called for removing the insane parts of the brain by a surgical process called a lobotomy, and the other involved trying to shock people sane with electricity.

"They put wires against both sides of the head and turn on a switch," said Josh. "I heard that the machine went haywire on a woman over in Cessna and completely burned up her brains."

"Stay out of trouble so they don't do any of that to you, Josh," Will said.

Birdie, despite having his eyes glued on Janice, heard Will's warning and said, before Josh could respond, "They won't do anything to Josh because he ain't going back there either, are you, Josh?"

"Yes I am, Birdie. You're OK now; you'll be fine."

"I don't get it," Birdie said. "We're friends, we'll make a great life—better than that awful one back at the asylum."

Josh had nothing more to say. Not now, not at this particular moment. Will Mitchell knew, too, that not going back to Somerset was not a possibility. But Josh's mind was a jumble of confusing thoughts. He was still uncomfortable with the spectacular atmosphere of the Harvey House. He hated not being able to read the menu. He wondered again how soon the bushwhackers called the police after he and Birdie turned up missing. Maybe they did nothing. Was Birdie right to be so scared about somebody looking for them? Josh suddenly feared what they might do to him when he went back. He hoped nobody blamed Streamliner for his and Birdie's escape. Or Lawrence. No matter what, at least Lawrence wouldn't have to sit through a Centralia massacre act anytime soon. That was the deal. God, how awful it would be to have part of your brain cut out. Or be forced to endure the electric-shock thing. He had been told by a bushwhacker with a cousin who worked at the Kansas State Lunatic Asylum over at Osawatomie that they were already doing it to everybody there. Only a few— ten or twelve—had had the treatment so far at Somerset, including that woman in Cessna. As far as Josh had heard, at least. They'd probably have done it soon to Birdie.

Janice arrived with breakfast, their several plates skillfully—magically—balanced on her left arm and hand. In addition to being beautiful and charming, thought Josh, she was really good at her job. Josh spread soft butter over all three of his pancakes, which were so hot they were steaming and so large they filled a whole regular-size plate. He poured on maple syrup from a little white porcelain pitcher that had *Fred Harvey* written across it in red script, as if it had been personally autographed by Mr. Harvey, whoever he was. He must be an important and lucky man to have such a wonderful place named after him. Better than being a baseball player, who only gets his signature on a Louisville Slugger.

While Josh and Birdie filled their mouths with food, Will Mitchell watched with a look on his face that showed real pleasure. He clearly was enjoying bringing such an experience to these two escapees from Somerset.

Birdie finished his eggs and bacon and toast in a matter of a few very quick minutes. Josh was only halfway through his stack of pancakes and not paying attention to much of anything else when he noticed Birdie's eyes fluttering back and forth between open and shut. Eating had made him sleepy.

Josh said to Will Mitchell, "Maybe you should talk to Birdie so he'll stay awake."

"Nope. There's no time like the present to find out if the treatment worked," Will said. Josh thought there was an unusually insistent note in his voice. *Do it. That's an order.*

Ten seconds later, Birdie's eyes sprang open and he said, in a voice not much louder than a heavy whisper, "The blood. Don't shoot no more. No."

Will Mitchell quickly reached across the table and tapped Birdie lightly on the right temple with the heavy handle of a table knife. Like the syrup pitcher, it had Fred Harvey's signature etched on it.

The hit made Birdie silent.

Janice was standing there at the table. The smile was gone from her beautiful face, having been replaced by a sympathetic, worried frown. "Is he all right?" she asked. "Should I get a doctor—or a policeman? Why did you hit him like that?"

"I'm a doctor," Will said. "What we need is a place for some privacy, some special treatment."

"Yes, that's what we need," Birdie said quickly. "We need to go."

"Come with me then," said Janice.

So Will, Josh, and Birdie went with Janice to the back of the lunchroom, passing by the concerned stares of busboys and other Harvey Girls.

They went through an unmarked door and down a narrow hallway to some steps. At the bottom of the stairs, she led them through a large storeroom full of canned goods and boxes and crates of foodstuffs to a far corner, where there was a large mirror hanging vertically on the wall.

The mirror, it turned out, was attached by tiny door hinges on the left side. She pulled it open, away from the wall, and revealed a real door behind it, which opened to a dark room that was brimming with the mixed aromas of salt, pepper, cinnamon, and other spices. "This is our condiment and spice room, but nobody uses it much anymore except to hide out. One of the chief chefs—he's at the Harvey House in Chicago now—liked to come down here when he wanted to be alone, more or less. He was the one who put the mirror over the door to double-protect his privacy."

The room was windowless, not more than twelve feet square, and was furnished with an unfolded army cot, a straight-back wooden chair, a small table, and, against three walls, floor-to-ceiling shelves that contained a smattering of tins and jars of many different kinds of spices.

"You do what you need to do, doctor, and then you and your friends may leave on your own," said Janice. "You don't have to come back through the lunchroom to get out. Just turn the other way, go to the end of the hall, and there is another set of stairs—for employees—that will take you out near the main waiting room."

Josh and Will thanked her, Will giving her a couple of dollars for their breakfast—more than its actual cost.

Birdie took Janice's hand in both of his. "Once the doctor cures me of my ailment, I promise you will see me again," he said, as if he were delivering really good news to what he clearly assumed was a grateful young woman.

Janice's only response was an innocent smile and a slight noncommittal wave as she closed the door, leaving the three of them in the room alone with the smell of condiments and spices.

"I really must go soon to take out those tonsils, Josh," Will said, immediately after she disappeared. "Maybe the best thing would be for me to take Birdie with me."

"Yes, that would be a good thing to do," Josh said. "That way I can go back to Somerset and not worry about him."

Josh looked hard at Birdie, who shook his head rather casually. "No way," said Birdie.

"If you're really sick, come with me. If you're not, you can either go back to Somerset with Josh or off into the land of the free, Kansas City or wherever. I have to leave now—right now."

"I'm not going anywhere with either of you," said Birdie. "Not back to Somerset, not to some doctor's office in Kansas City. I want you to stay here with me, Josh."

Josh ignored him and spoke to Will. "Help me. At least try it my way. I can't leave him here like he is . . . it isn't just the closing eyes, either. He's been acting strange ever since we got here, haven't you, Birdie?"

"Just keeping a good lookout, that's all," said Birdie.

Will Mitchell looked at a pocket watch he pulled from a small pocket in his trousers and threw his hands up in a gesture of frustration. "All right, all right."

XV

RANDY

KENWOOD

1997

Randy Benton had promised a nice old retired Harvey Girl that he would deliver a message to a frail old escaped lunatic. He would tell Birdie Carlucci, "Thanks for the memories."

That was the thin reed of justification Randy clung to for making the forty-five-minute drive south to the small town of Kenwood this Saturday afternoon. Fortunately, he only had to use his reasoning on himself, because Melissa and the kids were gone for the day on a special guided tour of the Truman library and residence in Independence. Melissa had volunteered to be one of three parents to help chaperone the twenty kids who were members of their school's history club.

The county had contracts with five or six privately owned "group residences," mostly in nearby rural areas, where they placed feeble, destitute elderly people with mild mental problems who could not function by themselves. The program was part of a concerted effort a few years back to get homeless people off the streets.

The facility where Birdie Carlucci was living was a huge three-story white frame house that must have begun life at least a hundred years ago as somebody's mansion. Driving up and parking in the half-moon driveway, Randy figured there had to be at least twenty or twenty-five rooms in the place. The Kansas City social worker on Carlucci's case had told Randy there were eleven other in-need people living here. That meant there had to be a minimum of six or seven bedrooms, assuming there were no more than two in a room.

He was no expert on architectural styles, but the tall windows and wide porches struck him as being Victorian. There were several other houses of similar size and style in the neighborhood, all of them like this one having been converted to apartments, medical offices, and other non-single-residence uses. The telltale signs were the outside fire escapes.

A woman—fortyish, black, friendly—in a white dress greeted him from behind a small table just inside the front door and identified herself as the supervisor in charge. He had called ahead so she was expecting him.

"We've got him sitting on the big porch in back, all ready for you, Lieutenant," she said. "You'll have some privacy because everyone else is off on a group trip to the Southtown Mall. I have a quick question first. The social workers can't locate any family for Mr. Carlucci. In fact, we can't even find anybody with the last name of Carlucci anywhere in the Kansas City area—both sides of the line. Can you help us? Does he have any kin still around?"

"I honestly don't know. Have you asked him?"

"We have. Mr. Carlucci just shakes his head. The woman who came to see him claims she's not related and doesn't know of anybody who is."

"A woman?"

"A very ancient woman, walks with a cane."

"Short white hair, well groomed, thin, erect?"

"No, no. Bent over, long gray hair, plump."

"What's her name?"

"I have it here. We make everybody sign in—including you, by the way."

She opened a green book with the word VISITORS embossed in gold on the front and looked at the signatures. "Here she is."

Randy looked down at a tiny, light, wavering signature of a person named Hilda McIlhenny.

"How did she know he was here?"

"You're the detective. Why don't you ask him?"

Randy signed his name in the visitors' book and then followed the woman's instructions to go through the main hallway straight through to the porch at the back of the house.

There was Birdie Carlucci. They had him ready for Randy, all right—so ready that Randy might not have recognized him in a different setting. Somebody had cut his hair and shaved off his beard and generally scrubbed him up in such a way as to completely change his appearance. He had gone from being a wild-looking, sickly, homeless bum to a clean, normally sickly, ghostly pale old man.

"Mr. Carlucci, it's me, the police officer who found you at Union Station. Good morning," Randy said.

Birdie Carlucci was moving back and forth slowly in a white wicker rocking chair. He looked up at Randy, smiled, and said, "I'm rocking. Rocking is what they did at Somerset. That's what we were doing when I first met Josh. There wasn't a thing wrong with me but they didn't know that, so I had to do what they said. Rock, rock, rock, they said. So rock,

rock, rock I did. Rocking and sweeping the floors with big heavy brooms were the main things to do there. That's what Josh said, and he was right."

Carlucci spoke like a different man—a real person—without long pauses between words and phrases. His voice was extremely weak but what he said was firmly stated and easily understood. Whatever else, he had already learned how to talk again.

"There's another chair like mine over there," he said to Randy. "Drag it over and join me, if you like."

Randy liked. He grabbed the other rocking chair and moved it to a spot alongside Carlucci.

"Rock, rock, rock," Carlucci said.

Randy began rocking in sync with the other man's slow rhythm. Both of them were facing out toward a big backyard that was filled with the laid-out wickets of a croquet game, a couple of outdoor barbecue grills, and several wooden picnic tables and chairs. Beyond a high-wire back fence there was a field of what appeared to be early growing alfalfa.

"I have a message for you, Mr. Carlucci," Randy said, after a minute of rocking. "Janice Higgins said to tell you 'Thanks for the memories.' She said you'd get it."

The chair next to Randy did not change rocking speed. "She was so good to me," Carlucci said. "At the beginning, I wouldn't have made it without her. I think I loved her, and I *know* she loved me. They all did."

Rock, rock, rock.

"I understand you've had a woman visitor here?"

"Her name was Hilda Owens when I knew her at Somerset. She loved me too."

"Was she a patient?"

"No, no. She volunteered to read poetry to patients. Playing around with her is what forced Josh and me to leave—to escape. I'd only been there a few days, but I had already had enough. They hit me in the head with bats and did all kinds of other awful things. I had already decided to get the hell out of there."

Inmates didn't just decide to leave insane asylums—any more than they left jails or prisons. But Randy didn't interrupt.

"Hilda was married to a banker in town. Josh said they would probably kill me if I didn't leave. He saved my life. Josh is a wonderful man. He witnessed a massacre over at Centralia. That's what did him in—in the head."

Randy remained silent. There was no way he was going to tell Birdie that it was most unlikely that his friend and savior witnessed a massacre or anything else at Centralia.

"Did you find Josh and tell him where I was?"

"Not yet, Mr. Carlucci, not yet."

Without a beat, Carlucci continued. "Hilda's husband threw her out of his house and out of town and she came back to Kansas City. I ran into her at Union Station shortly afterward. I saw her coming out of the women's waiting room on her way to catch the 3:15 Milwaukee Road to Minneapolis. She came back to see me there at the station a few times—until she married another banker. There were other women, too. Some came right off one train, like, say, the Santa Fe Chief from California, looking for something to do before catching their connecting one, say a Wabash local to St. Louis. I was their something-to-do between trains."

Randy could not imagine how a guy could pick up women at a train station and get them onto his cot in a spice-smelling room in the basement.

"I know it's none of my business, but—I'm curious—how did Hilda Owens find out you were here at this residence?"

"I called her on the phone they have here and asked if she wanted this back." Carlucci held up his right hand and with his left unfurled a pink kerchief. It was tattered, torn, and dirty—but intact. "She gave this to me at Somerset. When she came here she told me to keep it. In sixty-three years, I never went anywhere without it. It was in my pocket when you arrested me."

"I didn't arrest you. I *found* you."

"Same thing. Look at me now, sitting on a porch rocking like a Somerset lunatic. I'm not a lunatic and never was."

Never was a lunatic, Mr. Carlucci? Sure thing, old man. What Randy said was, "You're being taken care of here, Mr. Carlucci. You weren't in very good shape when I came across you."

"I miss Union Station." Were those tears in the old man's eyes? Was he really crying over no longer being confined to a cramped, smelly little hole in the wall of a deserted, falling-down train station? But it hadn't always been that way.

Randy said, "I understand, Mr. Carlucci, I really do because I grew up loving Union Station too. I thought it was a magic place, an entirely different world. I always saw it a bit like going to church, a cathedral where you didn't have to keep quiet, where you could smile and yell and eat ice cream—"

Randy stopped talking when he saw that the old man had turned to stare at him. His face was literally lit up by a grin that transformed him to somebody much younger, out of place at this group residence for the sickly homeless.

"Union Station was the most exciting building in my world too," said Birdie Carlucci. "I saw it as the place I'd go someday to get on a train that would take me on an adventure to a life far, far away from Kansas City, where there were dolls and dollars everywhere."

The old man stopped in midsentence, turned back to the front, and resumed rocking.

"That's the reason, of course, why it was such a pleasure and an honor to call it my home for so long," he said, his voice dropping in volume and verve.

Randy decided to ask some questions.

"What was it like at Union Station these last sixty-three years? How did you live? What did you do? Why didn't you just leave? Why did you stay there?"

Keeping his chair rocking and his eyes straight ahead, Carlucci said, "That's a lot of questions at once."

"You're right. I'm sorry."

"But I will answer them. It's been so long since I've really talked to anybody. I've missed that. I always enjoyed talking. I always had a lot to say. I need to have one last good spell of conversation."

Birdie Carlucci then started talking, not really to Randy at his side but to anybody straight ahead—in the backyard or the alfalfa field or beyond.

"That first day, Janice told me some men were around asking about a couple of guys who might have been Josh and me. Josh had already gone to get the train back to the asylum. I went downstairs to hide, maybe just for a few hours until I could think of a plan. I fell asleep on the cot, and when I woke up I went through the storeroom and found plenty to eat, and there was everything I needed so I decided to spend the night. I went upstairs and used the big men's bathroom off the waiting room. I sat in the waiting room for a while, like I was a passenger on the way to somewhere, picked up some newspapers that had been left there by passengers, and took a stroll up and down to a few of the tracks to see some trains come in and out. I really loved doing that. I wanted to ask people who they were and where they were going and why, but I didn't, not that first night. The next morning I ran into Janice coming down the employees' stairs. She was so pleasant, so beautiful. She came down a while later with some coffee and a plate of pancakes just like what Josh had the morning before—when I met her with Josh and the doctor. She asked where I was going now and I told her I wasn't sure and, who knows, maybe I'd still be here that afternoon when she got off if she wanted me to be. Of course, that's what she wanted. So she came to my room and we spent some time together."

"How did you get her to do it—just like that?" Randy asked. Something about this didn't make sense. Harvey Girls were famous for being prim and proper in accordance with strict rules that required certain ladylike behavior. For one of them to just jump into his bed—his cot, to be precise—like that seemed out of character.

"I asked her," Carlucci said. "That's how I got her to do it." The old man stopped rocking, looked over at Randy, and said sternly, "See here, young man, I haven't always looked the way I do now. I attracted women like mice to cheese . . . bees to honey . . . salt to fries. Believe it or don't believe it, that was the way it was."

Randy chose to believe it.

Carlucci resumed rocking and talking.

"Two days went by of moving around Union Station, checking out the trains, and reading discarded newspapers. Between what I found in the storeroom and what people left behind around the station and what Janice brought me, I was eating very well—certainly better than at the asylum and even better than at home—"

"Home?" Randy interrupted. "Where *was* your home in Kansas City? What neighborhood were you from?"

Birdie Carlucci didn't answer. He just picked up where he was. "So I decided to stick around a while. I didn't have any money, except some change from a dollar the doctor gave me. A week came and went. During the day I scouted out other corners and rooms in the station. There were hundreds of little places to lie down, to sit and read, to stay out of sight, to be away, to be safe. There was a little cubicle down in the basement, below the trains and the tracks, just off the pump room for all of the elevators. Somebody had put a comfortable chair in there. That worked well for me. The top floors were the best. There were tiny offices and special places. I spent many nights in a dormitory room with cots that was there for conductors and engineers and other trainmen who got stranded between trains. Nobody used it much, so I did. That's where Janice and I met a lot. It was right above—way above—the Harvey House. There were narrow stairs up against the east wall that you had to climb to get up there. When anybody did see me I always acted like I was a crewman on a train, on his way to someplace that mattered. I knew all the trains pretty soon, so it was easy to make up one for me that sounded right to the person I ran into. I went for walks outside the station. I even went down Main all the way to downtown, strolled like a banker by the hotels and the department stores, and saw streetcars and fancy women on the streets."

Carlucci took a breath and sighed. Randy seized the pause to ask, "You said earlier there wasn't anything wrong with you; you weren't a lunatic. What were you doing at Somerset?"

If the old man heard the question he gave no sign. He went on with his story.

"My real life at the station began when I found a book that was at least three inches thick. Somebody left it behind on a waiting-room bench. It was called an almanac. In a few days I knew the capitals of all the states and all the countries of the world. I knew their average annual rainfall and average family income and the names of all of the presidents and vice presidents of the United States. Then I learned all the members of the House of Representatives and the ninety-six senators and the governors and lieutenant governors of the states. I knew how many votes every candidate for president got from the beginning of elections. I memorized the Declaration of Independence and the preamble to the Constitution. I knew the crest records of the Mississippi and Missouri and Kaw rivers. Before long, there wasn't much I didn't know. By the time I finished reading that almanac and memorizing everything I wanted to, more than six months had gone by: eight or nine months, probably—maybe a year, now that I think about it. I got lucky, because before I finished the almanac, I found a Bible on a bench. Josh had told me that the guy who had my bed at Somerset before me was named Jesus. Not *the* Jesus, the one from Nazareth; this one was from Chillicothe. Josh said he had memorized the entire Bible, so I thought I'd see what *I* could do. I read it from cover to cover several times. Most of it didn't make sense the first time, so I kept reading it until it did and then until I knew it by heart. Now I know the Bible as well as Jesus of Chillicothe."

Carlucci stopped rocking. He turned to Randy and said, "Name a verse from the Bible. Any verse."

Randy was not a Bible person. His relationship with the Bible had been only in passing from his having attended Sunday school in Winston and, now, going with Melissa and the kids to a Methodist church in the neighborhood.

"Anything . . . maybe something from Matthew, Mark, Luke, or John," Randy said. For the first time in his life, his ignorance of the Bible was an embarrassment. "Whatever, Mr. Carlucci."

Carlucci shook his head. "Those four are too easy." He closed his eyes for a second, opened them, and said, "I'm thinking about something from the Old Testament, from Samuel. Do you know the Books of Samuel?"

Randy's silence was his answer.

"He spoke a lot about friendship," Carlucci continued. "In One Samuel, chapter twenty-two, verse twenty-three, he said, " 'Abide thou with me, fear not: for he that seeketh my life seeketh thy life: but with me thou shalt be in safeguard.' Did I quote the passage correctly?"

"Yes, sir," Randy said. He, of course, had no idea if it was from First Samuel or First John, or anyone else. It could have been from a fairy tale or a Hallmark greeting card, for all he knew. And clearly Birdie Carlucci realized that. He was playing with the unversed cop from Kansas City.

The rocking and the talking out into the backyard resumed.

"An awful thing happened only a couple of weeks after I'd been there. In November, a policeman—his name was Fanning, according to what I read in the newspapers—came into the Union Station. He was drunk and out of uniform, but he had his gun and he started threatening people. He went down to one of the tracks, where he shot and killed another officer who was trying to stop him. It turned out that Fanning was on duty the morning of the massacre and never got over believing his fellow officers blamed him for what happened. I heard all the commotion that night and saw them take out the dead officer on a stretcher and Fanning in handcuffs. Do you know the story?"

Randy said he had read about it recently in a book—Jules Perkins's book. "You witnessed the massacre itself, isn't that what you told me the other morning?"

All Randy heard from Carlucci was the sound of his chair rocking: *bump . . . ta, bump . . . ta.*

Carlucci, again ignoring Randy's question, picked up where he had left off:

"I went to the man who ran one of the restroom cleanup crews at Union Station and asked him for some part-time work. Occasionally he gave me a job mopping floors. He never asked me where I came from in the morning, and I never told him. Nobody ever asked me where I came from. There were always so many people in the station, coming and going. I also was careful to keep up my looks, unlike the others who hung out around the station. They were bums. I was not a bum and I didn't look or act like one. I made a little money from the mopping, enough to get an occasional haircut in the station barbershop, and I picked up some clothes— free of charge—from a Salvation Army place not too far away. Once they knew I could recite the Bible from memory, they gave me anything I wanted, including the use of their washing machine and an iron and ironing board. I also found an easy way to get into the station's lost-and-found room down next to the big baggage room in the basement. I never took anything important or valuable, only a few clothes. I made me a good life. Josh loved to read in the library, and now I was just like him. Before Somerset, I had never read much of anything, even in school. But now that was my main thing to do. I found other books lying around the station after the almanac and the Bible, some about war and crime and love. The Salvation Army also had some books.

"I stayed up on what time it was with the big clock between the lobby and the waiting room, I stayed up on what day it was by reading the dates at the tops of the newspapers. But even I was surprised one day to realize two years had gone by since I left Somerset with Josh. You can go up on the sixth floor and see the record I kept."

"Record of what?"

"My life at the station. It's in the big hallway leading into the dormitory room. I'm going to nap a few moments."

Carlucci kept rocking and looking straight ahead. But soon his eyes were closed, the chair was still, and he was asleep.

Randy decided to stick around until the old man woke up.

XVI

WILL

SOMERSET

1920

It was a new bushwhacker named Pete who finally prompted Will Mitchell to leave Somerset. Pete claimed to have been a professional baseball player—a right fielder—for the Philadelphia Athletics before turning to what he called *loony labor*. He was one of what Will discovered were hundreds of itinerant men who traveled the country with the weather and their whims, working as attendants at state insane asylums.

"This is the tool of my trade, doc, a Ty Cobb special," said Pete, the day he arrived at Somerset. He was holding a baseball bat—a Louisville Slugger—in his hands out in front of him. Will knew about these magnificent instruments of white ash. Every boy did. "It worked great hitting the ball out of the park, and it works great hitting loonies out like lights."

Will, who had played baseball in high school, was appalled. "I don't want you using that on any of our patients," he said to Pete, a bald gorilla of fifty or so who stood at least six feet four inches tall and some two hundred fifty pounds deep.

"I already have the play-ball sign from the big shots here to use it. But don't you worry, doc, 'cause I always wrap a little piece of something soft around the butt of this bat. That's so as not to draw blood or make scars. That way all it'll do is draw some attention and put out some lights in loony heads."

Before the first day was over, Will saw Pete hit three patients in the head with his bat. That night, Pete and his bat went through two or three wards, helping sleepless patients fall asleep. Josh did not escape his whack because this was before he and Will had had their Centralia revelation in the library. Now Josh was past needing such violent assistance to go to sleep and had, with Will's encouragement, already begun his regular Centralia performances in the auditorium.

But the other patients were regularly hit and hammered. Will raised steady and increasingly hot protests about Pete's batting to Dr. Mayfield, the superintendent, and anyone else who would listen. Not only did they not stop Pete, but it wasn't long before most of the other attendants bought baseball bats of their own to use on the patients. Replica autographs of famous major league baseball players like Ty Cobb were burned into the heavy part of the bats. One of the bushwhackers got a Rogers Hornsby, another a Honus Wagner. Soon the term *Somerset Sluggers* was born and became part of the asylum vocabulary.

The sound of those padded bats slamming against the heads and bodies of human beings, lunatics though they may have been, provided the last push for Will Mitchell. He still had ten months to go on his two-year commitment to the state health department, but that was too bad. One morning after watching a poor soul have his head nearly torn off by the swing of a bat, he decided he had to get out right away.

"I'm leaving this place in the morning and never coming back," he said to Josh—as a secret—the afternoon of his decision. "You are my one and only proud accomplishment, Josh."

They shook hands.

"Thanks for making it possible for me to have a life in this place," Josh said.

"I wish it meant you could leave here and have a normal life somewhere else, far, far away from here . . . but that, of course, is not possible."

Josh said nothing. He didn't have to.

The next morning, just before six, Will threw his few belongings into a small tan leather suitcase his father had given him as a college graduation present. He hid the case in some bushes near the front gate and then, as usual, went to make his wake-up rounds.

His first stop was in a second-floor ward office station where he knew there was an attendant with a newly bought and outfitted Somerset Slugger at the ready. His name was Amos.

"Can I borrow that Honus Wagner bat of yours for a few minutes?" Will asked. "I've got a guy downstairs who needs some help concentrating."

"I thought you disapproved of these things," said Amos, surprising Will with his use of a word as long as *disapproved*.

"If you can't beat 'em, join 'em, is what I always say," Will replied in as buddy-buddy a way as he could manage.

Amos handed Will the Honus Wagner slugger.

Will walked down one flight of stairs to where he knew Pete was on duty.

Holding Amos's bat down by his side, he approached Pete, who was seated at a desk reading something. Probably a dirty comic book, Will thought.

"Good morning, doc," Pete said, looking up. "You got a slugger there with you? I can't believe it."

"If you can't beat 'em, join 'em, is what I always say," Will said.

With Amos's Honus Wagner in both hands, he raised the bat and, in two swift back-and-forth swings, whacked Pete's head from both sides, knocking him out cold and sending him sprawling on the floor.

He laid the bat down across Pete's stomach, walked quickly to the front door of Old Main and out onto the gravel pathway, retrieved his suitcase, and then continued down Confederate Hill to the Somerset train station.

A few minutes later, he was seated comfortably in a chair car on the Kansas City Southern's morning train, flying north toward Kansas City as straight as the crow flies.

XVII

JOSH AND BIRDIE

UNION STATION

1933

Josh motioned for Birdie and Will to take a seat on the cot, while he grabbed the chair and pulled it up close, facing them.

"I'm now going to tell you Streamliner's awful story," Josh said to Birdie. "I will do it as if I was him—as if it happened to me. And I want you to repeat it after me, sentence by sentence, like you're telling it—like you are Streamliner too."

"That doesn't make sense," Birdie said.

"Maybe so, but just do it," Will said impatiently. "It's either that or somebody's going zap your brain or slice a little piece out of it someday—whether you need it or not."

Birdie reflexively threw his hands to his forehead. Then he looked at Josh and said, "Let me have a few minutes with the doctor here—you know, in private."

"I can't do anything for you, young man," said Will Mitchell. "I really am not that kind of doctor."

"OK with you, Josh?" Birdie asked, ignoring Will. "Just for a minute?"

Josh figured there was no way he could say no to that. He knew from his own experience how helpful and good a man Will Mitchell was. If Birdie wanted to talk to him alone, so be it.

Will Mitchell was shaking his head, but Josh said, "I'll be right outside," opened the door, pushed the mirror forward, and stepped out into the large storeroom.

Josh decided to take a closer look at an open bay of what looked like canned foods—soups, beans, juices. Next to it were shelves ten feet high of bread and rolls. . . .

He heard a noise behind him and turned to see Will Mitchell coming out of the inner room.

"He's going to be fine," Will announced, his voice as loud as if calling a train over the PA and his hands raised high over his head.

"That can't be," Josh stammered. "You were only in there together a minute or two."

Will motioned for Josh to come back into the little room with him.

Inside, Birdie was lying on the cot, his legs stretched forward, his arms down along his sides. There was no cover or mattress on the cot, which was made of dark green canvas.

"This thing smells like mustard," Birdie said.

Will said, "Close your eyes now, Birdie."

Birdie's eyelids flicked up and down several times before staying shut.

"Are you all right, Birdie?" Josh said. "Will said you were going to be fine. Is that right?"

"I'll bet you he'll be asleep—like normal asleep—in a few minutes, if not seconds," said Will.

Birdie didn't react with either a word or a movement. But his eyes remained closed. They had been that way now for at least thirty seconds.

Will put a finger up to his mouth. Stay quiet, please, Josh—that was the message.

Josh and Will did not move or make a sound for a full minute. Two minutes, three minutes.

Then, after Will again took out his watch, they left Birdie sleeping, carefully opening the door, moving the mirror aside, and then gently closing the door and letting the mirror swing back in position behind them.

Will offered Josh his right hand. "Great to see you again, Josh," he said. "Now I really do have to go."

"What did you do to Birdie?" said Josh. "You said you weren't a lunacy doctor—"

"Birdie and I worked out a little treatment that was special only to him, and it worked."

"What treatment?"

"It doesn't matter. People can snap into lunacy and they can snap out of it. The important thing is that it worked and you can leave him with your mind at ease."

"How do you know the snap will take—will last forever?"

"I know it as well as I know I have to leave right this second and take that little girl's tonsils out."

Will removed a well-worn brown leather billfold from his right hip pocket. "I'm going to give you some money to give to Birdie once he wakes up. He'll need to catch a trolley or a bus to somewhere, maybe his home—wherever it is. Don't worry about him anymore."

Josh thanked Will for his generosity.

Will gave Josh a one-dollar bill for Birdie. "Now, what about you, Josh? You're definitely going back to Somerset?"

"Of course I am," Josh said. "I just didn't want to go until the kid was all right. I can't imagine what you did in there in just a couple of minutes."

"Even in the world of lunacy medicine there are occasional miracles, Josh. Trust this one, and trust me. I know you have to go back. Now go in peace of mind." Will extended two dollar bills toward Josh. "Buy yourself a ticket on this evening's southbound Flying Crow."

Josh didn't take the money. "I'm sure I can steal a ride—"

"Take the money, Josh, for God's sake. Go back as a real person with your head high, not as a cowering thief. Are they likely to punish you for escaping—hurt you badly with a ball bat or something—when you get there?"

Josh said he didn't think so but he couldn't be sure. He took the two dollars.

"Thanks for whatever you did for Birdie," Josh said. "I don't know what it was but . . . well, I really couldn't have left him the way he was."

Will made a move to go.

"They said at Somerset that he was an insincere lunatic, not a maximum one," Josh said. "But I didn't believe it, do you? You should have seen the way he was acting when we first got off the train. And don't forget Birdie wouldn't have been sent by some judge or doctor to Somerset in the first place if he hadn't been some kind of real lunatic. I never saw a sane person there."

"I did, I think. I saw a few that seemed to be there because somebody paid some administrator to take them. Who knows?"

They shook hands again and embraced, and Will disappeared at a half trot in the direction of the employees' stairs, the way Janice had said for them to leave.

Josh pushed the mirror aside and returned to the little room to watch Birdie sleep.

Whatever else might be going on, Josh knew Birdie wasn't faking *that*. The kid was snoring.

XVIII

RANDY

KENWOOD

1997

The old man slept for more than twenty minutes.

"What kind of policeman are you?" he asked Randy, within seconds of opening his eyes again.

"I'm a detective, a lieutenant. I handle mostly armed robberies—holdups, shootings."

"You're not working on the Union Station massacre, are you?"

Randy laughed. "No, sir. That's history and *only* history now. Nobody but professors and book writers are working on that anymore. I'm just curious about it."

"I was there."

Randy held his breath, but Carlucci said nothing else. "So you said. What did you see, Mr. Carlucci? I'd love to hear your story."

"I was paid to be there that morning."

"Who paid you? Who were you working for?"

"Some guys—mostly Italian, like me."

"What were you doing for them?"

"Hawking newspapers—kind of. They hired me because they knew I knew the place; I went there a lot with my cousin, who was a real *Star* boy. They wanted somebody who knew Union Station."

Randy stopped rocking. "You said something the other morning about Pretty Boy Floyd and Righetti. Did they hire you? Were they there? Did you see them?"

"I'm not saying any names. Never have, never will."

"Was your not wanting to be a witness the real reason you went into hiding that day at Union Station?"

Carlucci smiled. "I guess a person could figure that would be the last place they'd look for me—at the scene of the crime."

"Who, Mr. Carlucci? Who was looking for you?"

Birdie Carlucci stopped rocking and looked over at Randy. "The guys who hired me, the cops, J. Edgar Hoover and his G-men: I figured everybody was looking for me. I was a kid, I was scared, I didn't want to be found by anybody. That's why I was sent to Somerset in the first place."

"I don't get it," Randy said.

Birdie smiled and resumed rocking. "After the massacre, the guys who hired me were afraid I might talk and because I was a kid they didn't want to kill me, I guess, so they paid off some big shot at the asylum to stash me there until it all blew over. That was the plan. At Somerset, nobody but the guy they paid off knew I was a phony, so I had to fake being nuts for everyone else. I was doing pretty good at it, *too* good, so after a few whacks to the head and my fooling with Hilda, Josh got me out of there."

The old man's voice cracked—and then fell silent. Randy couldn't tell if it was from weariness or the subject.

After another twenty or thirty up-and-back rocks, Carlucci spoke again. "Have you ever seen Somerset?" he asked Randy. And when Randy said he hadn't, Carlucci was off again. He had his voice back.

"From a distance it looks like a castle in a moving picture, but up close it was a place for making people crazy. You were supposed to be that way when you got there, but Josh said if you weren't, they'd make you that way. He was right. I wasn't there long enough to find out much except about the rocking and the sweeping. But I knew I'd really be crazy if I'd stayed there long. They hit my head a lot. They also made me run around naked and spend a lot of time in a bathtub. So, like I said, with Josh's help, I went back to Union Station and made me a life there. It was great. I had the trains and the people and the books. The most exciting times were when there were wars. I loved watching the men in their uniforms come through in troop trains. They were all so full of fight and noise and whiskey. I entertained three WACs at one time during World War Two. They had missed a train connection to Chicago and had to spend the night at Union Station. I invited them to my room, and it was cozy and wonderful. I did my part for the war effort, was the way I saw it." Carlucci laughed. So did Randy.

"The Korean War didn't bring so many troops through the station. I saw in the papers it wasn't as big as World War Two. I saw Harry Truman forty or fifty times, I guess, coming or going from the station to Washington and other cities. He always walked through like he was going somewhere but he usually took the time to wave and smile at everybody, including me, when we were close enough for us to see each other's eyes. Even after he was no longer the real president I saw him as *my* president. He was a great man. I read about it in the newspapers when he died. That was a very sad day for me."

There were tears in the old man's eyes now, Randy saw. But he kept talking.

"Many of the trains quit running once the war in Vietnam started. I never really understood that war, but it upset a lot of people. That was when the really bad times began for me. You ever hear of a train called The Flying Crow?"

Randy said yes. He knew about that long-gone Kansas City Southern passenger train.

"Josh and I came to Union Station from Somerset on the Crow—that's what the railroad people called it."

"Yes, I remember you told me that the morning I found you."

Birdie Carlucci ignored the interruption. "The Crow was a beautiful sight coming into Union Station on Track Three; that was its usual track. For a long time, I went down there to watch the Crow arrive every morning, thinking maybe Josh might be on it. I always believed that someday he would leave Somerset and come back to Union Station—even if it was just to connect with another train going somewhere else. When he did, I wanted to be there. I wanted to apologize to him."

"For what?"

"For faking it, for lying to him. He thought I was a real lunatic, but I wasn't—never was. I saw the first day I was at Somerset how some of the loonies seemed to scream from something awful they'd seen in their lives, so I decided that's what I would do too. I'd really seen something bad— the Union Station killings—and I wanted the attendants and the doctors to think I was a real nut. Josh thought I was real, too. I never told anybody about the Union Station thing, of course, until I told Josh at Union Station later. Nobody at Somerset knew what kind of awful thing I was pretending to see when I was screaming. Josh tried to help me from the beginning. Later, I let him believe his doctor friend had snapped me out of it. That was at Union Station."

"Was the doctor named Mitchell, Will Mitchell?" Randy interrupted.

"Sounds about right. I was only with him a short time. I came away liking him because I got him in private away from Josh for a minute, told him I was a fake lunatic, and asked him to help me convince Josh I was OK. Josh was trying to get me to memorize another man's horror story about how his sister got torn to pieces by The Flying Crow, and I didn't want to have anything to do with it. The doctor said OK because he'd already pretty much figured out I was a phony. I was trying at first to keep

Josh thinking I was too crazy for him to leave me alone so he wouldn't go back to Somerset. That was an awful place but, to be honest, I also wanted to be with him."

The old man took several quick, short breaths. Randy had a million questions but decided not to ask them.

"That doctor said he knew all I was up to was getting a free breakfast at the Harvey House. So he told Josh he had performed some kind of quick miracle on me and I closed my eyes like I was normal and, before I knew it, I went into a real, normal sleep. The only other thing that was real was my looking around for cops and mob guys when Josh and I got to Union Station that morning. Josh thought I was just nutty. But the rest was lies. I shouldn't have done that to Josh. He was trying to be my friend. He *was* my friend. I shouldn't have done that."

Randy had no idea what most of this was about. A little girl torn to pieces by The Flying Crow? But he decided to let it be.

"Josh never did show up, but it gave me something to think about when I woke up each morning, something real and lovely to do no matter what else. *Are you coming this morning, Josh?* My plan was to tell him everything and then see if he would forgive me, and then I would try to talk him into staying there at Union Station with me. I was going to show him around, let him see all the books I had collected, and maybe he would see how great a life it could be for him. I also thought having him there would be great for me too. I got very lonely at times, particularly every Christmas Eve. There were always great red and green lights and baby Jesuses and wiseman dolls and a huge Christmas tree in the grand lobby. There was Christmas music playing and little old men in Santa suits and people carrying presents. I watched all the hugging in the grand lobby and down at the tracks when families were coming together or parting before or after Christmas. But none of it was for me. If I were a poet I'd write something about being in the middle of thousands of songs and lights and words and laughs but none of them for me. I was alone. My birthday—November twelfth—was even worse than Christmas. I'd wake up and say, Happy birthday, Birdie. But then I'd go through the whole day without anybody else saying that to me. I tried one year acting like November twelfth didn't come. I went from November eleventh to November thirteenth, not reading the papers in between. It didn't work. How can anybody wipe out his birthday? You ever been alone?"

The question was for real. "Nothing like what you're talking about, I guess," Randy said. It was as honest a response as any he had ever given. *Alone.* He would never again think of that word in the same way.

"I sometimes talked to passengers and people hanging around, but never for long and never in a way that was really personal. Most of the bums that slept on the waiting-room benches were drunk or living in other worlds. I didn't want them in mine. Most of them got picked up regularly by the police and were thrown in jail for a while. I didn't want any part of that. It was my choice. I can't blame anybody. Alone was what my life was. I figured all I needed to make it better was one person. I didn't need a crowd or a family, just one person to be with. Josh would have been perfect. But he never came."

Randy tried to picture this poor man meeting the same train day after day, year after year. On reflex, he said, "I'm so sorry, Mr. Carlucci. That must have been terrible for you every day."

Carlucci raised his left hand in a movement of dismissal and said, "That's what friends do."

At least Randy understood that part of the story very well.

"The Kansas City Southern pretty much replaced the Crow as their main train with a new streamliner called The Southern Belle. Then, in 1967, they killed the Crow off altogether. I went down to Track Three to watch its last trip in from Texas and Louisiana. It had its diesel engine and it was painted in the yellow, red, and black colors of the Kansas City Southern. There were only a dozen passengers on it and a few other people around—nobody important or special. I couldn't get over why nobody was there to make a fuss over the last trip of The Flying Crow. I really cried that day. I went into one of my rooms and cried. Things like the Crow and people like Harry Truman shouldn't be allowed to die, should they?"

Randy said he agreed about that.

"I was also probably crying too because it meant that Josh would never ride The Flying Crow out of Somerset."

Carlucci paused, took a long breath.

"The most awful part about when the trains stopped running was that it also meant they stopped taking good care of Union Station. First, parts of it were closed off, including the whole sixth floor, which by then had been turned over to some people who collected toy trains. They had them running around on tables. Some fool took out all the wooden benches in the waiting room and replaced them with colored seats. From the newspaper, I read about the material they used: plastic—something new, I guess. They looked awful. The Harvey House closed and other restaurants came and went until one day there weren't any at all. That meant I had to go outside to get something to eat. The Salvation Army was fine, and occasionally I found things people had thrown away. The newsstand closed and so did the bookstore. Fewer passengers meant fewer books left behind in the waiting room for me to read.

"I woke up one day in the eighties—late in the eighties—and realized I was almost the only person left. They weren't keeping the place clean or painted. Water leaked through from the roof every time it rained or snowed. The big clock quit working. The passenger trains were no longer run by railroads but by the government. The passenger cars and engines were all silver with red, white, and blue trim. Everything was alike. Then, one day, they weren't here either. No trains, no stores, no girls to love, no people at all, no nothing. Just me. Only me.

"The thing I missed the most at first was the noise. There was nothing more exciting to me than the commotion of all those people traveling or working on the railroad, moving around that big old place like they were in a separate town—a different world from everything outside. I was scared for myself and how I was going to live. I thought about giving up, of surrendering, of just going to a policeman and announcing, *All right, here I am. I'm the escaped lunatic from Somerset. Birdie. Yeah, yeah, Birdie, that's me. And I saw the big massacre here, too.* I actually walked out of my room a couple of times on the way to do that, but I always stopped before I got to the top of those basement stairs. I wanted to be where I was; I wanted to stay at Union Station.

"I went for a long, long time without seeing one person in the building. I heard a watchman go through every morning and again in the early evening, but I was always able to stay out of his sight. I kept moving my things around from the offices—all of them empty—on lower floors and my other places. There were several rooms with huge fans that had been used to blow the smoke from the trains up and out of the station. I was always looking for a better place than my little room. But finally I had to go back there because it was the only space that stayed pretty warm in winter and fairly cool in summer. Strange, isn't it? Why would the condiments and spices room be the best place in the whole Union Station for me to stay comfortable?

"Also, animals started getting in the station. I heard them and saw signs of them in the daylight. I was never sure what they were. I had read so many books by then about wild creatures coming into homes and buildings that I'm afraid I let my imagination scare me. I guess the only things that came in were mice, rats, squirrels, and stray dogs and cats. But sometimes late at night I believed I saw big monsters with green tails and ragged teeth—things like that. I got to a point where I only left my room when I had to. Going to the bathroom was the worst part. All the real ones in the station—I'll bet there were fifteen of them by the time you counted those for offices—had been closed or shut down. So that meant I had to go outside to do everything, and I had to do it at night so nobody would see me. I am not proud of what containers and methods I used to dispose of my waste. But I had no choice."

Carlucci fell silent.

Randy saw that the old man was breathing hard.

"I've worn you out," he said. "I'm sorry."

"I've worn *myself* out," said Carlucci, taking some deep breaths. "I'm talking for myself as much as I am for you. Josh said he told his Centralia story from a stage at Somerset for himself too. I never heard him tell it, but he said it was his cure for going to sleep."

Again, Randy chose to say nothing about Centralia.

They sat in silence for at least two or three minutes.

"Josh was my best friend. Have you had a lot of best friends?"

"Yes . . . sure. Well, maybe not what you'd call a lot." Randy remembered Willie Rogerson in high school. He was his best friend then. In college, there was Johnny Semple. Right now? Well, not anybody at the department who he'd call a *best* friend. There had been partners when he was on patrol he thought of as best friends. The best of the best, of course, was Mack Gardner. They had come into the department together as cadets and gone up through the ranks side by side until Mack moved slightly ahead, having made captain last year. Technically, he was now Randy's supervisor. That had cooled things off. There had been a time when they went fishing together down in the Ozarks, took their kids to Chiefs and Royals games, exchanged secrets and fears. . . .

"Josh was the only one I ever had in my life—you know, a real best friend. And I was only with him for three weeks. Yeah, it wasn't very long from the time I got to Somerset until he left on the Crow to go back that night from Union Station. I guess it proves time doesn't have much to do with best friends."

At first, what the old man said sent a blast of unbearable sadness through Randy. But, then, the more he thought about it, he decided maybe having a real best friend for three weeks wasn't so bad. Some people probably went through the whole of life without ever having one for even a day. He knew some cops like that.

"Josh couldn't still be alive, could he?" Carlucci asked Randy. "Are you good at mathematics?"

My aunt Mary doesn't think so, Randy almost said.

"I know he couldn't be," Carlucci continued. "I wonder where they buried him?"

"I'll find out for you, Mr. Carlucci." The words came out of Randy's mouth automatically. Only after speaking them did Randy wonder how he would find that out. And why? Why would he go to any trouble for this old man?

Carlucci was no longer rocking. Neither was Randy.

Within a few minutes, Carlucci's breathing got weaker, and as it did so, his eyes closed. Soon, he was once again in a real sleep.

 On his way out, Randy asked the woman at the table, "Why is the old man so weak? He seems to be worse now than when I found him."

"He was terribly malnourished when he came and he doesn't eat much, but that's not really it, of course. Between his condition and the medicine, it's inevitable that he'd be declining—and rather fast."

"What medicine?"

"Well, first he's on a couple of the new miracle medications designed to keep him mentally stable."

"There's nothing unstable about his mental condition that I can see. He just entertained me with a full report of his life and times. It seems to me his mental condition actually seems stronger and healthier—*more* stable."

The woman waved him off. "The doctors interviewed him, got his case history. He's a mental patient, a sufferer of traumatic shock syndrome—something like that. He's being treated for that with medication. Why do you cops care about this guy anyhow?"

Randy raised his eyebrows and did not answer.

"That's nothing compared to the heart thing, of course," said the woman, as if she was telling Randy something he already knew.

"What heart thing?"

"He's got degenerative heart disease. He's fading, failing. I assumed you knew."

Randy felt his temper rising. "Why isn't he in a hospital being treated?"

"There is no treatment except a transplant. And I don't think a mentally deficient man his age is ever going to get one. What do you think, Lieutenant? Where would he be on your priority waiting list for a new heart?"

At the *top,* you idiot! he screamed—silently.

XIX

JOSH AND BIRDIE

UNION STATION

1933

Josh awoke to a few moments of disoriented panic. It was only after he took in a full whiff of cinnamon and other spicy smells that he remembered exactly where he was and what was happening.

There was Birdie on the cot, his eyes still closed, his breathing peaceful.

How long had they been sleeping? How much time had gone by? Was it still morning, or had afternoon or nighttime come?

How much longer before The Flying Crow departed Union Station for Somerset and points south?

The sight of Birdie brought back Will Mitchell's idea about Birdie's not being a real lunatic. Josh knew better. Will was wrong about that. But Josh thought Will was definitely right about one thing. Maybe I, Josh, should be in charge of the Somerset lunatic asylum.

He would have laughed out loud at his own joke, but he didn't want to wake Birdie. Not yet. Will's comments aside, there was no telling how long it had been since the kid had had a natural sleep like this.

Josh had fallen asleep himself shortly after he returned to the cozy closed warmth of the tiny condiments and spices room. He dozed off while sitting in the chair, watching Birdie in tranquil slumber.

Josh was not a routine creative dreamer, not somebody who woke up remembering and being prepared to talk about something new or special—nightmarish or pleasurable—he had just dreamt. He went to sleep every night reciting his ritual about Centralia, and every morning when he woke up it was still Centralia that was on his conscious mind.

"I slept." Birdie was awake. He spoke the words calmly, softly, but in a tone of routine acceptance. *Of course, I slept.* He sat up and set his feet on the floor. "Your doctor friend really did do it, Josh," Birdie said. "He's a genius and so are you, for calling him to come over here. You should be running Somerset."

Josh remembered the word *groundswell* from a book he had read on the early history of Missouri. There had been a groundswell of support for making Jefferson City the state capital. Here now was a groundswell of support for putting a lunatic in charge of a lunatic asylum.

"You have saved my life, Josh."

Josh handed Will's dollar to Birdie.

"Let's go someplace, Josh," Birdie said. "Yeah, yeah. Let's get on a train and go as far as it will take us. We can jump on one the way we did on The Flying Crow. Maybe one of the Santa Fes to California. We can keep flying as straight as the crow flies."

Josh shook his head. "I have to go back to Somerset. Will gave me some money for the train, so I can go legal." He stood up. "Let's find out what time it is and when the train goes and buy me a ticket."

"I don't get it," Birdie said. "You're as sane . . . as cured . . . as I am. You can be free too."

"I can't ever be free," said Josh, moving to the door in a way that said there would be no more talk about the subject. "After you, sir," he said to Birdie.

Like Will, they followed the Harvey Girl's instructions for leaving the storeroom area, emerging at the top of some stairs into the noise and commotion of the main waiting room near Track 1 on the east side.

Birdie carefully covered up his face as much as possible again with the hat and collar. He also left Sister Hilda's kerchief tied around his neck. Josh didn't think it was a sign of craziness anymore. By now, there really might be cops looking for two Somerset escapees. He looked up at the big hanging clock between the waiting room and the grand lobby. It was fifteen minutes after four o'clock! It was hard to believe they had been down in that storeroom sleeping for so long.

"Pretty Boy Floyd spotted again!"

Somebody was yelling above the crowd's sound, which suddenly disappeared. This was big news. People were listening.

"Seen by cops in Toledo!"

It was a newspaper boy, coming from the newsstand in the grand lobby, holding a paper in one hand, more under his other arm.

"Hunt for Union Station killers continues!"

Several people rushed over and lined up to buy a paper. One of the first customers was Birdie, his head and face down. He got 95 cents in change back for his dollar bill.

He rushed back to Josh with a copy of the *Kansas City Post* and they looked at the front page together, standing by a wall in the waiting room.

The letters in the headline across the top were so large they took up a fourth of the page: PRETTY BOY SEEN! Underneath, in smaller type, it said: LANDLADY FINGERS KILLER FROM PHOTO.

The story said Floyd and Adam Righetti, his partner in crime and in the Kansas City massacre, had been on the run, many times barely eluding capture. Their trail had been picked up in Toledo, Ohio, where they had been living with two identified women. J. Edgar Hoover, the director of the federal government's Office of Investigation, said his top agent, Melvin Purvis, was in hot pursuit and vowed that Floyd would be taken "dead or alive." The Kansas City police chief was quoted as saying the search for possible Floyd-Righetti confederates "in and around Kansas City" was also continuing "at an unprecedented speed and intensity."

There were large prison-type mug shots of Pretty Boy Floyd and Adam Righetti in the center of the page.

"I have to get out of here," Birdie said, rather too loudly, it seemed to Josh. A redness had flashed into Birdie's face. Josh was happy to see that nobody around noticed anything. This was a train station. The people here weren't paying attention to much more than their own business. There were trains to meet or catch, baggage to check, meals to eat, cigarettes and magazines to buy, shoes to have shined.

Josh told Birdie to go on.

"You sure you won't go with me—fly away with me somewhere?" Birdie said.

"I can't do that, Birdie."

Birdie said he'd at least wait until Josh bought a ticket for The Flying Crow to Somerset. He kept his back to the people in the waiting room and motioned forcefully for Josh to go. "Go get your ticket!"

There were too many ticket windows, each marked with the name or symbol of a railroad or specific train or the type of ticket available—unreserved coach, reserved coach, sleeping car, today's trains only. It was very confusing. Josh looked for the Kansas City Southern. There were several windows for the Santa Fe and its trains. There was the Alton. Chicago Great Western. Frisco. Wabash. Three or four windows for the Missouri Pacific. Milwaukee Road. Katy. Union Pacific—five windows. Burlington. Rock Island. Finally, there was the Kansas City Southern. Its single window had over it a foot-wide flying crow emblem that was identical to the electric sign on the rear of the train this morning.

There were five or six people already waiting, and as Josh went to the end of the line, something most unexpected happened. He was overcome by a paralyzing feeling of dread, and it got worse the closer he got to his turn to buy a ticket.

"If you want to catch the Crow you'll have to get a move on," said the agent, the second Josh arrived at the window. He was in his late forties, wearing a white shirt, black tie, and red vest.

Josh couldn't speak. He heard what the agent had said and knew there were people in line behind him, wanting also, no doubt, to go on The Flying Crow.

His brain was aching. He really had to return to Somerset. Staying with Birdie didn't make sense. Birdie himself didn't make sense. That snap treatment Will had done certainly went fast and easy. *Too* easy? Was he an insincere lunatic? Why did that newspaper upset him so? There was no other place for Josh to go. *There was no other place to go!* After all these years, he doubted if he had any kin. Even if he did, it was unlikely they would claim him. And even if they did, the asylum and sheriff people would find him and his life would be over.

"A ticket to Somerset, please," he said to the ticket agent. The aching was over. He had no choice.

"One way or round-trip?" The agent was clearly exasperated, but he was allowing it to show only in his face, not his words.

"One way."

In less than a minute, Josh had his ticket and change—the fare was $1.10. The agent told him to proceed to Track 3, where the train was due to leave in ten minutes, and barked "Next!" to the customer behind Josh.

Birdie was right where Josh had left him. He seemed to be mumbling things about the Union Station massacre that Josh couldn't hear well enough to understand.

"Have a great life, Birdie," Josh said.

Birdie broke into tears and grabbed Josh in a tight embrace. "I don't think I can but I'll try . . . I'll try," he said.

Josh knew Birdie's tears were real.

Suddenly Josh wanted to cry himself. He was worried again about Birdie, about leaving him here by himself. But Will Mitchell had promised the kid would be fine. Will Mitchell could be trusted. Thank God for Will Mitchell. Birdie would be OK. Yes, he would be fine.

Josh really did have to go. He had a flying crow to catch.

XX

RANDY

KANSAS CITY

1997

Instead of being large, overstuffed, loud, and self-important as Randy had unfairly imagined and expected, Jules Perkins was sophisticated, trim, smooth, cool. But he wore a small black leather holster on his right hip. There was no weapon in it, but the message was, I'm one of you, Lieutenant.

No you're not, buddy!

But Randy couldn't yell that. Perkins had written in the preface to *Put 'Em Up!* that his version of the Union Station massacre saga came directly out of 20,000 pages of the FBI's own files on the case. Perkins had obtained them over a period of several months through a Freedom of Information request.

Randy needed Perkins and his files because they were the last stop. There was nowhere else to go in the search for Birdie Carlucci's story.

Randy had already confirmed what the woman at the Kenwood residence unit had said. There were no Carluccis living in or around Kansas City. A further check with the public library's computerized phone and city directories of the past turned up the fact that there never had been. Plenty of Carls and Carltons and Luccis but no Carluccis.

He had then gone to a computer in the police department's records office and typed in the name *Birdie Carlucci.* Nothing came back, meaning there was no record of an arrest or a witness or incident report in Kansas City proper or the metropolitan area—Kansas and Missouri—involving anyone named Birdie Carlucci. There were also no Carluccis in the police files.

He had looked for Birdie's name in the index of every book on the Union Station massacre he could find, including Perkins's. The listing in *Put 'Em Up!* went from *Caffrey, Raymond J.* to *Christman, Earl.* No Carlucci in between. And there was no Birdie in the *B*'s.

He also went through several true-crime-type write-ups on the Internet and the library's cross-reference system of old newspaper stories. None had a listing or a mention of anybody named Carlucci or Birdie as a witness or anything else connected to the massacre and the investigation that followed.

That was why Randy, after waiting impatiently for six weeks, was sitting now in the large Ward Parkway home of Jules Perkins, the world's number-one expert on the Union Station massacre. The house was a two-story mansion, one of many along the fifteen-block tree-lined parkway that ran southwest from Country Club Plaza, Kansas City's oldest and most elegant shopping area. The city's richest and best-known people had traditionally lived on Ward Parkway, and for the most part that was still true. Perkins's house was south of the mansion Tom Pendergast lived in before going to federal prison in the forties for insurance fraud. A star pitcher for the Kansas City Royals now lived a block farther south.

Randy, like most everyone else in Kansas City, knew the writer's story. Perkins had worked briefly as a reporter in St. Joseph, Missouri, before going to law school in Kansas City and becoming a criminal lawyer and then the well-known and prosperous author of crime novels he was today. *Put 'Em Up!* was one of his few books of nonfiction. Perkins's twenty-plus novels were mostly about the Italian mob's alleged influence on gambling, prostitution, city hall, and most everything else in Kansas City in the late seventies. Perkins's real money and prominence came from the hit television series KANSAS CITY, which was based on the books. The hero was a former assistant district attorney who served seventeen years in prison for strangling his beautiful wife after he discovered her in bed with a mob gunman who was suppying her with cocaine. Upon release from prison, the hero became a private investigator and a crusader dedicated to eradicating organized crime from Kansas City. Randy enjoyed the TV series more than the books.

The six-week delay in Randy's being able to see the great man was because Perkins was away as writer-in-residence at a college in Oregon.

"I'll give you my time and my sources on one condition, Lieutenant," Perkins said to Randy. They were seated across from each other at a long library table in Perkins's study, a majestic room of leather-covered furniture, dark woods, and hundreds of books. The walls were mostly covered with floor-to-ceiling shelves, black-and-white photographs of cops and lawyers, and framed copies of covers from Perkins's many books.

Perkins stated his one condition.

"When we're through, you tell me what this is all about. It's a bit unusual for a cop to be running down leads on a crime that was committed sixty-four years ago, even one as important as the Union Station massacre."

If you've got something that truly resolves it once and for all, I want to know what it is. I've spent almost ten years on this mystery. Deal?"

Randy was caught. He wanted this man's help and information. But he also wanted to protect Birdie Carlucci's privacy.

"Deal," he said. One thing at a time.

Randy knew from *Put 'Em Up!* that while there was good evidence from the FBI files that Pretty Boy Floyd and Adam Righetti were probably not involved, there was nothing conclusive on the identities of the other possible gunmen. That remained the major mystery. Another hoodlum of the times named Verne Miller was a major suspect, but he had not been tied to it beyond a doubt.

Perkins, in his book, had pretty much determined what happened that day out in front of Union Station. Two or possibly three armed men were waiting outside to spring Jelly Nash as he was being taken from the train to a car for the drive back to Leavenworth. They had not come with the intention of killing anybody or even of firing a shot but just to flash their tommy guns, yell "Put 'em up!" at the escorting cops and federal agents, and speed away from the scene with a freed Nash. But one of the lawmen sitting in the backseat of the officers' car accidentally fired a shotgun, blowing off the back of Nash's head and igniting a frantic and confused firefight that cost four more lives.

The main theory on the identities of the gunmen was that they were Miller and some locals who had been either hired or persuaded by mob friends of Nash to do the job.

"OK, what do you want to know?" Perkins asked Randy.

"Was there anybody connected to the case in any way named Carlucci, Birdie Carlucci?"

Perkins put his thin fingers to the sides of his head, which was barely covered with a few carefully combed strings of black hair. Perkins was thinking. Randy figured his age at somewhere between fifty-five and sixty. It was hard to tell for sure. Clearly, some of his enormous book and TV earnings had been spent on his hair, if not his face.

Now Perkins was shaking his head. "I don't remember any such name, but let me check. If he was involved, I'll have it here somewhere. I had a secretary organize all eighty-nine volumes of the FBI files under a very good cross-reference system."

Eighty-nine volumes? Randy was impressed.

Motioning for Randy to keep his seat, Perkins moved first to a desk in a corner of the room and typed some things into a computer. "All names, dates, and pertinent info is in here."

Within a minute or two, Perkins was again shaking his head. "Nothing. No Carlucci, Birdie or otherwise. Come see for yourself."

Randy stepped over to and behind Perkins. There on the computer screen was the same kind of listing blank that Randy had found in *Put 'Em Up!* There was the name of Caffrey, the federal agent killed on June 17, 1933, and then, as in the book index, somebody named *Christman, Earl.* No Carlucci.

"Done. There was nobody connected with the Union Station massacre in any way whatsoever who was named Birdie Carlucci," Perkins pronounced. "Now, please, Lieutenant, tell me what this is all about."

"Anybody with the first name or nickname of Birdie?" Randy asked.

Perkins shrugged but turned back to the computer. "That's harder, because most of these listings were only by last name. But I can cross-reference and see what I come up with. If the name were Jim or Bob, it would be more difficult."

After a hundred or so movements of his fingers on the keyboard and a few minutes, he said, "No Birdies."

Randy had watched the screen. He saw it before Perkins said it. There were no Birdies. "On witnesses to the actual massacre—right outside in front of the station itself. How many were there?"

"Hard to say accurately. One count would have it up in the hundreds. A lot of people decided afterward that they had seen things that would get them a little ink in the papers and attention at home. Some even went on to lie under oath at Righetti's trial. Hoover wanted them to see Righetti so they saw Righetti."

"What about real—confirmed, credible—eyewitnesses?" Randy was not through yet.

"Only a handful, apart from the surviving lawmen who were there, and most of them lied for Hoover too. For the real folks it was a normal busy morning, with taxis dropping off passengers and the like, but people were minding their own business. Not until the first shots were fired did anybody really turn to look, and by then it was pretty much over. Everything happened in a little over a minute."

"Any of those eyewitnesses a kid—a boy in his late teens?"

"White?"

"Yeah."

"There were some redcaps out front, but back then the feds and the cops didn't see black people as reliable witnesses."

Perkins went back to the computer one more time. Within only a few seconds, he said, "Nope. No young white male eyewitnesses. All of them were in their thirties or older—or were female."

Perkins stood and walked a few steps over to a large stand-alone four-drawer file cabinet against a far wall. The cabinet was made of a dark wood that matched the bookshelves and most everything else in the room. "Just for the sake of thoroughness, let me pull out a few of the actual files. It's conceivable something slipped through my system, although I doubt it."

Randy went with him to the cabinet. There were the eighty-nine files.

Perkins pulled open the top drawer, grabbed something from the front, and handed it to Randy. "You might get a kick out of seeing this anyhow—no matter what you're looking for."

It was a file, three-quarters of an inch thick, held together at the top by silver brads that had been stuck through holes from underneath and then bent down. Most police files are fastened the same way.

The FBI cover sheet said, in big black letters on white paper:

FILE DESCRIPTION
SUBJECT <u>KANSAS CITY MASSACRE</u>
FILE NO. <u>62-28915</u>
VOLUME NO. <u>1</u>

Randy lifted the cover sheet. There, in all its stunning historical significance, was a copy of the original telegram the agent-in-charge of the Kansas City office sent that morning, informing J. Edgar Hoover of the massacre.

DIRECTOR, UNITED STATES BUREAU OF INVESTIGATION, WASHDC=
OTTO REED CHIEF POLICE MCALESTER OKLAHOMA SPECIAL AGENTS
FRANK SMITH AND LACKEY WITH FRANK NASH WERE MET UNION
STATION THIS MORNING SEVEN FIFTEEN AM BY AGENTS VETTERLI
AND CAFFREY AND TWO LOCAL DETECTIVES. NASH WAS TAKEN TO
CAFFREYS AUTOMOBILE IN FRONT UNION STATION WHEN

UNKNOWN PARTIES BELIEVED FOUR ALTHO DEFINITE NUMBER
UNKNOWN OPENED UP WITH SUBMACHINE GUNS KILLING TWO
LOCAL POLICE OFFICERS CHIEF REED FRANK NASH AND SHOOTING
AGENTS CAFFREY IN HEAD FATALLY LACKEY SHOT RIGHT SIDE NOT
BELIEVED FATAL FRANK SMITH ESCAPED UNINJURED VETTERLI
NIPPED IN LEFT ARM LICENSE NUMBER OF SHOOTING CAR
OBTAINED DOING EVERYTHING POSSIBLE. VETTERLI.

Randy knew from having read Perkins's book that the license number turned out to be of no help in finding anybody.

"Keep looking if you want to, lieutenant," said Perkins. "Most of the first eyewitness material is in Volumes One and Two. I'll glance through the next couple just to see if something leaps out."

Randy turned the pages and read, and Jules Perkins did the same. After ten minutes, Perkins said he had something that might be of interest.

"There's some stuff here about a kid—a white boy. I had forgotten about him. I didn't have him in my cross-reference file because nobody ever came up with a name. A couple of the fairly reliable witnesses, including one of the surviving federal agents, said there was a kid walking in front of the formation with Jelly Nash and the officers that morning. He was a *Star* boy, they said, selling newspapers. And just as they came out the big east doors he raised one of the papers above his head. The theory was that he was in cahoots with whoever was lying in wait and was signaling them to get ready, *here they come!* Obviously, if true, the kid would know for sure who the gunmen were because he was part of their team. So everybody looked hard to find him afterward."

Randy concentrated on breathing steadily. "Who was the kid?"

"Haven't a prayer. If he existed, he disappeared. I mean, completely disappeared off the face of the earth. Nobody, not a soul in the FBI or the KCPD or anywhere else, ever got an ID or a lead on him, much less saw him or interviewed him. The *Star* had no record of such a kid working outside like that on that morning. Nothing turned up. Everybody, including me, finally decided he probably never existed. That's why I didn't put him in my book or cross-reference anything about him in the files. If he were real, let's face it, somebody would have come up with a name and the whole story by now. Of course, it's possible he was hired by some gangsters to be a signal lookout and they got rid of him afterward. Or maybe all that killing wasn't something the kid bargained for and he simply ran as fast and as far away as he could, on his own or with somebody's help. Who knows? And who cares anymore except me—and now you, lieutenant?"

Randy wanted out of here. He extended his right hand to Jules Perkins and thanked him for his time and patience. They had been at this now for almost an hour.

Perkins took Randy's hand and held it. "OK, now it's time for your part of the deal. What's up? Why are you here?"

Randy had had a few minutes to work on his story. "We had a woman in a nursing home who said a man—this Birdie Carlucci I was asking about—gave her a deathbed confession about having seen the massacre. The captain asked me to check it out if it interested me. I had just read your book so it interested me. That's all."

Jules Perkins squeezed Randy's right hand even tighter. "What did the dying man say, for crissake?"

"He said he was just a kid and he happened to be riding his bike south on Main that morning—you know, along the eastern side of Union Station—and he happened to glance up and see two men with high-powered rifles shooting down from the roof of the station into the front parking lot."

Perkins dropped Randy's hand as if it were trash. "That's impossible—and ridiculous. Slugs from pistols and tommy guns and pellets from shotguns were found at the scene, but no rifle slugs. Not a one. It didn't happen. I can't tell you the number of crazy stories like that the cops and the feds ran down. I did a few myself. There was a Travelers Aid woman who claimed she saw three nuns that morning right outside during the shooting who must have seen everything. She said the nuns were wearing those wide flying-white hats. Thousands of investigator man-hours were eaten up at convents and parochial schools all over the area looking for those three nuns. The woman made 'em up. I can't believe some dying guy used up his last breaths to invent some sharpshooters on the roof. It's nonsense. I would have expected KCPD detectives to have more pressing and plausible business to tend to."

Randy made one of those people-do-the-strangest-things kind of shrugs.

"Too bad your dying man wasn't that phony *Star* boy who was the lookout that morning—assuming there even was such a kid," said Perkins.

Randy responded with a smile and a nod as he closed the door behind him.

If he had been the type of person who was inclined to leap and shout for joy, that's exactly what Randy Benton would have done the moment he was outside on Ward Parkway.

Instead, he drove a few blocks south, turned down a street to a small park, stopped his car, went over to a bench, pulled out his cell phone, and called the group residence in Kenwood.

He recognized the voice of the woman who answered as the one who had handled his visit a few weeks ago.

"I'm just checking in—wondering how Mr. Carlucci is doing," he said, after identifying himself. "I was thinking about coming out today and paying him another visit."

"You're too late for that," said the woman. "He left us night before last."

"Left? Where did he go, for God's sake?"

"Either heaven or hell, but I don't know if it was for God's sake."

Randy felt something welling up inside him. Part of it was anger. He wanted to yell at somebody, throw something across the park—or out a window.

"I just can't believe it. I can't believe it."

"Believe it, Lieutenant. We buried him yesterday—at a cemetery out here."

When she didn't hear anything in response from Randy after several seconds, she said, "He went peacefully in his sleep."

Randy still said nothing.

The woman at the residence, clearly exasperated, hung up after saying, "You know something? Everything they say about you cops is right on. Is being weird part of the job description?"

Randy closed the cover on his phone and, with nothing conscious in mind other than to calm himself down, he started thinking back to when all this began. He went back a few days, one week, two weeks, a month, six weeks, more, until he came to that day of the Union Station inspection when he first met Birdie Carlucci. Or, more correctly, a man who said he was Birdie Carlucci. There was no telling now what his real name was or where he came from. Or what he was doing at Union Station on June 17, 1933. Or who, if anybody, he was working for. Or what he saw.

Randy figured that Carlucci—that old man—died ten weeks almost to the day after they found him cowering in the corner of the old Harvey House's condiments and spices room. Did he die like a fish does when taken out of water? Or like a crow does when he can no longer fly?

Ten weeks. If Jules Perkins hadn't been out of town and Randy had been able to talk to him earlier, maybe he really could have gotten the old man to talk, to clear up everything once and for all.

If Randy Benton had been a man with an explosive temper, which he was, he would have tossed that cell phone across the park as hard and as far as he could.

Which he did.

XXI

JOSH

SOMERSET

1933

Josh mostly kept his eyes focused on what was passing by his window from the moment The Flying Crow eased away from Track 3 and then creaked slowly out of the Union Station yards.

Go back as a real person with your head high, not as a cowering thief.

Those words from Will Mitchell were among many that reverberated with the clicking and swaying of the train as it picked up speed on its way south from Kansas City. Josh had a window seat just forward of center in the second of three chair cars. This was Josh's first ride in so modern and luxurious a railroad car. The few train trips he took before coming to Somerset had been in small, noisy, lurching, bare coaches. On this trip he found the seats, covered in a green material that resembled velvet, strikingly plush and comfortable. The brass door handles and silver chrome luggage racks, as well as the side and roof paneling of light beige wood, glistened with care and polish. This was definitely a head-high way to travel.

There had been only one disruption.

"You going to Texas too?" asked a stupid idiot sitting next to Josh when they left Union Station. "I'm going to hop a freighter in Port Arthur and work my way to Honduras or somewhere—who knows where." He was young, dressed in work clothes that looked homemade, not cleanly shaved or, from his odor, freshly bathed.

But who and what this man was didn't matter. At this moment, Josh wouldn't have wanted to talk to the fanciest, cleanest, smartest person in the world. His wish was to sit here and enjoy, second by second, minute by minute, what he assumed would be his last look at any part of the outside world.

So he only gave a quick glance and mumbled, "I'm just going to Somerset."

"Somerset? That's where the loony bin is, isn't it?" said the fool. "My mom always yelled she'd ship me off in a straitjacket to Somerset when I acted up crazy. Why you going to Somerset?"

Josh wanted his privacy, his moments of silence and thought, more than anything else right now. There were other seats where this guy could sit—two or three were unoccupied in this car alone.

"I *was* shipped off to Somerset in a straitjacket," Josh whispered, flipping his eyes up, down, and to each side in a way that he hoped made him appear weird and crazed. "I was released as cured a few months ago, but I've had a relapse so I'm going back before I kill and eat even more people."

It seemed to Josh that everything in and about the kid froze.

"I sometimes thought and acted like I was a lion," Josh added, still in a whisper. "I mauled people to death and then even ate parts of a few of them—the noses and ears are particularly tasteful."

His companion shot up from his seat as if he'd been given a hot foot and backed away down the aisle without saying another word.

Traveling straight as the crow flies, Josh returned to his thoughts and to watching the Missouri countryside pass by. He considered Will Mitchell's point about returning to Somerset as a real person. Not possible, doctor. I am not a real person, not anymore. What does it mean to be such a thing anyhow? Was that dumb kid who just ran away a real person? What about Streamliner? And Lawrence? The bushwhackers? How could a real person whack people in the head with bats? And the doctors? Shooting electricity through people and cutting out brains and looking at them to see what was in there to make somebody a lunatic?

No more thinking about any of that. Not now. Once back at Somerset, he would have plenty of time to consider such things, most particularly when compared to what the alternative was for Joshua Alan Lancaster. Somerset or death: It was that simple.

There, out the window, was a little schoolhouse. White. Wooden. No kids outside. They had gone home for the day and would be back tomorrow. Poor Streamliner. . . .

But that was something else he could think about some other day.

Birdie. What a quick, smart, delightful kid! He smelled so bad the first time we met, that day during rocking time. He'll do great as a real person in the world. With the girls for sure. They really do like him. Maybe he'll become a doctor, a great one like Will Mitchell. Or maybe a lawyer or a preacher. I would go to hear him preach. No, I wouldn't. Forget being a preacher. I don't like preachers. They're too sure of themselves. How can people be really sure of themselves in this world? There's so much that can go wrong. Or just different from what you planned, or hoped, or prayed. Maybe Birdie will write books. That's it! I wish I had said that to him. I would love to go into the library and pull down one of his books from the shelf and read it. I can't imagine knowing somebody personally who wrote a book. Wonder what Birdie would write about? Probably not anything too serious. Maybe he could write a love story about one of the girls he's known. Not Sister Hilda! Leave her alone, Birdie! Don't see her, don't talk to her—don't write a love book about her. . . .

"Hummer! Next stop Hummer, Missouri!"

It was the conductor, walking through the car. Josh had seen him only once, shortly after they pulled away from Union Station. He had welcomed Josh aboard, took Josh's ticket, punched it three times with the snap of a silver punch he pulled from a leather holster, and placed a small cardboard receipt on the edge of the baggage rack above. The conductor was a cheerful little man in a dark blue uniform and cap with a shiny gold K.C.S. CONDUCTOR badge. Josh decided not to ask if he knew about the lunatic at Somerset who got that special northbound Flying Crow slowdown and whistle-blowing every Thursday morning.

The Hummer station house was right in front of Josh's window when the train stopped. It was small, made of rough gray stone. Josh watched three passengers board and five others leave the train. One of the passengers who got off was a young woman in a long brown coat. A man in a gray suit and hat ran to her. They hugged, he took her suitcase, and they walked away holding hands. Josh had read about things like that in the Somerset library's books. He wondered what it would be like to meet a woman at a train station, hug her with all your might, take her luggage, and walk away with one of her hands in yours. Thinking about it didn't make him sad, only curious. He had a life at Somerset that was what he deserved and that was that.

The train began its slow, chugging creep away from the Hummer station.

As the building disappeared from his sight, Josh thought again to the incredible glories of the Union Station back in Kansas City. All of those people doing so many things at once, going to and from so many places on so many trains run by so many railroads. And the Harvey House lunchroom. It really was like a church. He had never in all his life had pancakes like those, and he knew he never would again. This had certainly been some incredible day since he left Somerset on the back of a train like this one.

Here came the conductor down the aisle from the front of the car. Josh had seen him out on the Hummer platform, assisting both the arriving and departing passengers. Now he was looking right at Josh. "Next stop is Somerset, sir." Sir? *Sir!* Doesn't he know I'm not a real person? Hasn't he figured out that I'm an escaped lunatic on his way back to the asylum? Was that the first time anybody ever called me *sir*? It was the flash of a thought and it passed. Because it didn't matter.

The conductor paused to take Josh's ticket receipt down from the luggage rack. "Please exit from the front of the car."

Josh promised to do so.

He tried to think of other things as he felt and heard the train slowing down. Somerset was just a few minutes away now. He so much wanted to leave this train, end this momentous day, with something special or different or new or unusual on his mind. Something more important than whether he had ever been called *sir* before.

"Somerset! Next stop Somerset, Missouri!" called the conductor, as he passed through the car again.

Josh stood up and followed him toward the front, as ordered.

His mind remained free of a new or important thought, and in less than a minute the train was stopped dead still in front of the Somerset station, a brown wooden building barely half the size of the one in Hummer.

The conductor put a step stool down on the platform. "Thanks for riding with us," he said, as Josh stepped on the stool and then off and away. Maybe Birdie could be a railway conductor. No, forget that. He'd be in trouble all the time for going after the women passengers.

Josh raised his right hand and waved. Good-bye, Flying Crow. The train began its noisy move out of the station on its way to Texas.

"Hey, Josh, bud! Is that you?"

Josh turned to see a guy in white coming his way. It was a bushwhacker. Well, here we go. But as he got closer he saw that it was Jack. Thank God. Jack, the good bushwhacker, the one from New Zealand who used his fists instead of a Somerset Slugger, a soft rope instead of hard leather straps.

"They all said you'd come back, but I didn't know," Jack said, once he got right up to Josh. He was carrying a small cardboard box of something he had clearly just bought in town. It looked like office supplies: pencils, rubber bands, and the like. The Flying Crow was gone, having left behind only the smell of burning coal and the blare of its whistle, growing fainter as it rode farther south down the track.

"Is that Birdie kid with you?" Jack asked.

Josh shook his head.

"They all said he wouldn't come back," Jack said, "but they said you had no choice."

Without another word, they walked off together across the tracks toward Confederate Hill and the asylum.

Josh looked ahead, and all he could see was the red bricks and turrets and white-framed windows of Old Main. The people of Somerset were certainly right to call it Sunset. It blocked out everything, not just the sun. Josh was struck by how big a building it was, larger even than the Union Station in Kansas City. That amazed him, now that he thought about it, and caused him to conclude that it's what a building is used for that counts, not the size. Size has nothing to do with being grand or beautiful.

Now, that was something new and different to think about, even if it wasn't very important.

"We already put a new guy—some bud from over at Springfield—in Birdie's bed in the ward," Jack said. They were walking side by side, almost nonchalantly, up the long curved gravel path alongside the main road toward the front gate and onto the asylum grounds.

"What about my bed?" Josh asked.

"It's waiting for you just the way you left it."

The arched white wooden gate was now in sight. It was wide and tall enough for a large truck to enter and was covered from the ground, up both sides and across the top, in vines of red roses. Someone might mistake it for the entrance to a park or a rich man's estate rather than a lunatic asylum.

Josh decided not to hold that thought. He decided to return to thinking about the sizes of buildings.

But Jack put a hand on Josh's shoulder. They were now ten yards away from the gate.

"Josh, there's one thing I gotta do before we go in there, and I'm betting you know what it is."

He would have lost the bet. Josh, his mind still not where it probably should have been upon returning to Somerset, had no idea what he was talking about. He had forgotten for a moment that he had to be a lunatic in order to stay alive.

Jack must have read that in Josh's reaction, because he said, "You're an escaped patient, bud. They'd never understand the two of us strolling in together like this. So I've got to make it look like I captured you. I need to use my restraining rope."

Josh made no effort to resist as Jack took his soft rope and wrapped it around around Josh's chest and stomach four times, holding his arms hard down against his sides.

"All right, then, bud, let's go."

They took a step forward together as Jack asked, "You know, several of us wonder a lot if you're really crazy anymore. You sure don't act it most of the time. Why they keep you here—"

Josh pulled his arms as hard as he could against the ropes. He rolled his eyes back in his head and screamed, "Let me go! I'm drowning in the blood! Let me go! Here comes Bloody Bill!" He sat down on the ground and kicked his feet like a child.

"Hey, there, Josh, I can't take you inside in the middle of you having a fit."

Josh put his head between his legs and screamed. "Bloody Bill Anderson's going to scalp me! Help me! Help me!"

"I don't want to hurt you, bud, but a job's a job."

Josh felt a jarring, painful blow from a soft fist to the side of his head. He blinked his eyes a few times, twisted his head back and forth, and, with Jack's help, stood up.

The fit had passed.

With Jack behind him, Josh walked on through the gate for the rest of his life.

XXII

RANDY

SOMERSET

1997

After several days of brooding, Randy realized he could never close his mind on the saga of Birdie and Josh until he went to Somerset, to see what there was to see.

So with the full knowledge and permission of Mack Gardner, his captain, he took a leave day and drove south for ninety minutes on U.S. 71 and a few connecting two-lane country roads to the town—and world—of Somerset.

Randy did have one problem blip with Mack before leaving. It was not about going to Somerset but about what to tell a *Kansas City Star* reporter who had picked up word about a dead homeless guy who'd been found at Union Station.

"He's apparently gotten on to much of the story, Randy," said Gardner, a dark thin man who, like Randy, jogged every morning and worked out to keep himself fit. "He's even heard something about the guy's claim that he witnessed the Union Station massacre. Can that be?"

They were standing in the open detectives area outside Mack's glass-enclosed office. Randy couldn't afford a loud exchange. He had to speak quietly, routinely—and quickly.

"That was just the crazy talk of a sick old man. Besides, I promised him, just before he died, that we wouldn't put out any publicity about him," Randy said.

"Why would you do something like that?" asked Gardner. "It's one helluva story, when you think about it. Even without the massacre stuff, here was a guy who claimed he lived in Union Station for more than sixty years!"

"I know the story. Forget it," Randy said. He spoke with dismissive authority, as if he were the captain and Mack was the lieutenant. "I gave my word. We have to honor it."

And Randy departed for Somerset.

A service station attendant in town pointed toward a hill—Confederate Hill, he called it—overlooking the town. "There's not much of the old hospital left," he said to Randy. "Go up to the first red brick building at the end of the entrance road. There's a state office in there. They'll help you out."

Within a few minutes, Harry Leonard, identified by a woman in the office as "our unofficial archivist and historian," was leading Randy down some steps to the basement of the red brick building.

"You trying to trace an old relative, Lieutenant," he asked, "or is it official?"

"It's official," Randy replied, and then added, "but it's also about a friend."

They went through a maze of pipes and fairly modern heating, cooling, and maintenance equipment to a door that Harry unlocked with a key—one of several he had on a large round silver ring.

"It's all in here—all that's left," Harry said. He had the look of an athlete, or at least a weight lifter. A man in his sixties, he wore his gray hair in a crew cut and clearly took very good care of himself. His stomach was flat, his arms hard and muscular.

They walked into a huge, dark, musty room that was full of head-high gray and green metal file cabinets and stacks of cardboard file boxes. After Harry had turned on some lights, Randy could tell this was truly, as they said upstairs, *the* ancient part of the building. The white wooden ceilings were high and in need of patching and painting, the plaster walls were gray and cracking, the floor was concrete, cold, slippery.

"When was your friend here?"

"For only a short time in 1933, I think."

"That was more than sixty years ago. The best and quickest way to start is by looking at the patient rosters. There's one for every year since this place opened in 1869. They're over here."

Within a couple of minutes, Harry had a long legal-size sheaf of white papers in his hand. They were stapled together at the top.

"Here's the roster—the official census, they called it then—for 1933. What's your friend's name? Is he still alive?"

"No, he just died. I think his name was Carlucci, Birdie Carlucci."

Harry looked down at the roster. "You think, huh? Let's see now. The list's arranged alphabetically, so it should be easy to spot him. Once we confirm he was here we can go for his file. If he was here for only a few weeks . . ."

Harry was shaking his head.

"What is it?" Randy asked.

"There's nobody named Carlucci on this list as being a patient at Somerset Asylum for *any* length of time during *any* part of 1933. Here, look for yourself."

Randy went through the list of typed names. In neat columns after the names were the Missouri county where each person came from and then three designations, either Stearman, Beech, or Cessna. Harry explained that those were the names of the three wings of the institution.

Those wings were long gone. Randy had marveled at a large color photograph of the original building that was hanging in the lobby upstairs. Birdie Carlucci was right about its looking like a castle in a moving picture. It was huge, almost as large as Union Station. But, as Harry explained, all that remained of the gigantic complex now was this center section of what had been called Old Main. The first three of its four floors had been modernized to house a regional office of the Missouri State Health Department and now sat at the entrance of an industrial and business park. The vast asylum grounds here on Confederate Hill had been sold by the state to a developer on condition he rehabilitate and maintain this one small portion of the institution for use by the state. Harry had told Randy all of this on the walk to the basement. He also said he had worked at the state hospital at Somerset, as it was called then, until it was shut down in 1992. Now he was a caseworker for the health department, on the verge of retirement.

Randy couldn't find a Carlucci on the 1933 roster either. There was somebody named Christopher William Carlsen and a Richard James Davenport, but nobody—alphabetically—in between.

"I'm almost certain . . . fairly sure, at least . . . that he was here then," Randy said to Harry.

Could the old man have made up the whole thing about being at Somerset Asylum as well as the massacre witness story? Sure, he could have. But what about Janice the Harvey Girl and the other little things?

Harry let out an exasperated breath. "This would not be the first time somebody who was here didn't turn up in the records. They tinkered with the records all the time. Somebody must have decided they didn't want there to be any trace of your friend Carlucci. Why was he here just a short time?"

"He escaped."

"Never located afterward?"

"Not until recently."

"That's it, then. An administrator, probably in 1933, didn't want to have anything in writing about somebody who had escaped and was still at large. He could always claim the guy was never here: 'Hey, look at my records!' "

"That doesn't make sense."

Harry laughed. "Making sense was not what this place was all about back in those days, Lieutenant. Was your friend involved in some- thing . . . you know, controversial? Criminal?"

"Why? Would that matter?"

"Well, I was told they sometimes used the asylum to hide people."

Randy's mind was working fast. "Like who?"

"Oh, gangster types mostly, back in the thirties and forties. My dad—he used to work here, too—said the Pendergast boys in Kansas City and their Italian mobsters used to send people here to get lost for a while. It was a perfect place to hide somebody. They paid off the asylum administrator to drop them into the patient population without even telling the doctors or any other staff they weren't really crazy."

Bingo! That was it. There *was* a phony newsboy signalman for the Union Station gunmen. And it was Birdie Carlucci, or whatever his name was. Afterward, with the help of the people who hired him, he was sent to this place.

Yeah, yeah. Maybe. Who knew? Who would *ever* know?

Birdie died in peace; let him rest in peace too, thought Randy. "Nope," was his answer to Harry about whether his friend Carlucci was involved in anything criminal.

But as he said it, Randy quickly flipped the pages of the roster until he came to the name of Joshua Alan Lancaster.

He showed the name to Harry and said, "How about this guy? Could you find his file?"

"Joshua Alan Lancaster. When was he admitted?"

"August 1905."

Harry Leonard smiled. "You don't have to be a genius—or a cop—to figure out this one could not have been a friend of yours. If you weren't a cop I wouldn't go any further with this without a court order. These files are under lock and key to protect people's privacy. Even to this day, there are folks who are not tickled about word getting out that they're kin to people who were inmates in a state lunatic asylum. I made an exception for that first guy of yours, but now you're asking about another—"

"But I *am* a cop, and Lancaster was the best friend of *my* friend."

"All right, all right. Did the guy die here?"

"Most likely, yes."

"When?"

"I have no idea . . . other than that it was after 1933."

Harry reached down in the file cabinet and pulled out several more census lists. He handed a bunch to Randy and kept an equal number for himself.

"We'll look at each year until his name disappears. The year before would be the year he either died or left the institution. It's under that year his patient history would be kept."

Randy, covering himself with flying dust as he went through the lists, saw that Josh was still there in 1935 . . . '36 . . . '37 . . . '38 . . . '39 . . . '40. . . .

"Here we go," said Harry, holding up the papers he was checking. "He was on the 1967 roster, gone in 1968. That means, assuming everything's in order, we should find his file in 1967."

And within a few minutes, they did.

With Harry's permission, Randy took it over to a corner, sat down on a stack of boxes, and began skimming through it.

Most of the early section in the two-inch-thick file was already familiar to Randy. That had to do with Josh's murdering his family in 1905 and the circumstances of his committal to Somerset. A sobering notation, usually in large type, appeared on many of the pages about Josh's future. For example, one of them read: THIS PATIENT, IF PRONOUNCED SANE, MUST BE TURNED OVER TO PRISON SYSTEM. DO NOT RELEASE UNDER ANY CIRCUMSTANCES!

Randy's eye zeroed in on a write-up signed by Dr. Will Mitchell in 1920. Mitchell declared Josh Lancaster to be "making remarkable progress in overcoming his inability to sleep normally." He recommended that Lancaster be "allowed and encouraged" to assist his fellow patients who suffered from similar maladies.

The rest of Josh's Somerset story was mostly about routine matters and about how helpful he had been to various doctors and attendants. A major exception was a four-sentence account of his being "recaptured" by an "alert attendant" following an "unauthorized absence" from the asylum for a full day in 1933. The key sentence was: "The patient Lancaster, using devious methods, left the asylum grounds with another male patient." That was Birdie. That had to be Birdie. He was here; Harry probably had it right. Some on-the-take administrator had simply eliminated Birdie Carlucci from the asylum's main records.

Another most interesting series of entries were those through the years expressing the opinion that Joshua Alan Lancaster appeared to be cured and thus probably no longer insane or suffering from acute lunacy. Shortly after each such entry from a doctor or attendant, there would be another about a sudden recurrence of his lunacy, usually marked by uncontrollable fits and an inability to go to sleep. It didn't tax Randy's cop mind much to figure out what that was all about. Birdie's friend Josh had clearly decided that life at Somerset Asylum definitely beat being hanged.

It was at the end of the file—toward the last of its hundred or more pages—that Randy took sharp notice. Josh Lancaster became ill with what was diagnosed as pneumonia and died peacefully in his sleep on February 12, 1967, at the age of seventy-seven.

He died peacefully in his sleep.

A minister was with him at his death. There was a printed form headed DEATH REPORT that had a line labeled *Disposition.* Someone had written, *Buried in Unknowns Section of cemetery.*

Randy stood up and went to Harry Leonard, who had remained in the basement and was passing the time by rearranging some old attendant personnel files.

"Why would they bury this man as an unknown?" Randy asked Harry with some edge in his voice. "They knew his name."

"He must have been without visitors or interest for several years, so when he died they declared him an unknown and just had a preacher come out from town and read the Bible over the body in a box at graveside. It was simpler. Otherwise, they'd have to go to the trouble—usually fruitless, anyhow—of trying to locate next of kin."

"Can I see his grave, or where his grave is? Where's the Unknowns Section of the cemetery?"

"It's under one of the new warehouse buildings over and down by the Kansas City Southern track," Harry said. "I think it's directly beneath the Wal-Mart distribution center, to tell you the truth."

Randy started counting to himself. At twelve, he said, "How in the name of decency was that allowed to happen?"

"When the development started four years ago, they moved the head-stones to a cemetery in town. Each is only a foot long and three or four inches wide and all they have on them are numbers. No names."

"What do you mean, they moved the headstones? What about the . . . you know, the bodies, the remains, whatever's left in the ground?"

"Somebody decided moving them would be too expensive and not worth the trouble. Who would have known or cared anyhow? So they left them there and built over them."

Randy was ready to go now. He *had* to go before he said or did something really stupid. His curiosity—his obsession—with two men who had lived in an insane asylum before running away to Union Station more than sixty years ago was rapidly coming to an end.

Then, as he arranged the Lancaster file to hand back to Harry Leonard, he noticed a final piece of paper stuck in at the end. It was a typed statement by somebody clearly not that proficient at using a typewriter, because it was filled with type-overs, mark-throughs, and misplaced capital letters.

TO WHOM IT MAY CONCERN

I was called by an attendant at the Somerset hospital to come speak to a patient who was near death. The patient had requested that he be allowed to say something important to a minister of the Lord before passing on to his reward. I went to the hospital and to the bedside of Joshua Alan Lancaster, a patient I knew only as Josh from my frequent visits to service the spiritual needs of hospital patients and staff.

In a weak but clear voice, Josh asked that I listen to what he had to say and pass it on in whatever fashion I desired to God in Heaven. I promised to do so.

He then told me that on a Sunday morning when he was fifteen years old his father ordered him not to go to Sunday school. The father, disturbed and angry, said the whole family—his mother, two younger brothers, and a sister, as well as himself—could not go this morning. But Joshua disobeyed his father, ran out of the house to their church in town some two miles away, and went to Sunday school anyhow. Upon his return to his house after church more than an hour later, he found his entire family dead. Each and every one had been brutally stabbed to death with a pitchfork. His brothers and sister were in one room, his mother was in the kitchen, and his father was in the back bedroom.

Josh said all but his father were lying on their backs, clearly victims of someone's unspeakable anger. His father was lying on his side with the spokes of the pitchfork still in his chest. Josh concluded that his father must have killed the others and then killed himself by falling or throwing himself onto the fork. In the fury that followed this supposition, Josh yanked out the pitchfork by the handle and repeatedly thrust it into various parts of his father's lifeless body, stopping only after he had succeeded in burying most of the metal part fully into the body's flesh. He said he was crying and yelling and begging for God's mercy as he did so. He said he believes with certainty that he lost his mind at that time.

He said he told the town marshal and everyone else that he, Josh, had been the killer. He said he told that lie out of shame for his father but, most compellingly, out of his own personal guilt for having been the only member of his family to survive and for having run away to church that morning. Maybe, had he obeyed his father and stayed at home, he might have been able to prevent the massacre of his beloved family. I made a vain attempt to placate his feelings of guilt. What he said finally was that what he knew now, as he faced death, was that he wanted his Lord and Savior to know that it had not been he who had taken the lives of his family. He committed crimes that fateful Sunday morning but not the crime of murder.

Josh died within the hour after his discourse to me. I returned to the hospital the following afternoon to preside over his burial service. Later that day, while studying God's Word at my desk at the parsonage, I concluded that there was a value to putting this deathbed statement down on paper, to be made a part of the record of one man's tormented life. I did so, in keeping with Josh's last wish, after first reporting Josh's words to God in Heaven. I did this in direct communication through prayer.

In the name of the Father, the Son, and the Holy Ghost,

R. W. Lanpher, pastor
First Church of the Nazarene
Somerset, Missouri
February 13, 1967

Randy sat back down. He read the statement again—and again. That year, 1967. Didn't something else happen then too? Yes, Birdie Carlucci said that was when the Kansas City Southern killed The Flying Crow.

Now he really did *have* to go.

But Mack Gardner was right. It was one helluva story. Randy had come across many strange and compelling tales in his years as a police officer but never one like this. Here was a kid who confessed to a horrible massacre he didn't actually commit but was perhaps driven insane anyhow. Maybe not, but he spent most of his life in an asylum. Another kid was driven insane—maybe or maybe not—by having participated in and witnessed another massacre. If Birdie Carlucci really was just sent here to hide out by some Kansas City gangsters, he wasn't really nuts. But on the other hand, sane people don't live in train stations, even great ones like Union Station, for sixty-three years, do they?

Randy thanked Harry Leonard, handed him the file, and stepped toward the stairs.

Then he caught sight of a large alcove in a corner behind the stairwell. He asked Harry what was in there.

"Some equipment from the old days," said Harry. "There used to be a maintenance guy around who pack-ratted what he thought might be in a museum someday. I made sure none of it was thrown out."

Randy had trouble imagining his kids' school history club and tour busloads of other happy children and chaperoning parents filling up parking lots to see relics from an old insane asylum. But, that issue aside, he was curious about what kind of stuff had been saved.

There were a couple of shelves of books, most of them appearing to be bound copies of official documents and writings about Missouri history, particularly from the Civil War period. There were at least three or four just about the Centralia massacre.

And there was a Bible, a very old version covered in soft black leather that had begun to deteriorate.

Randy reflexively grabbed it off the shelf and opened it. There, at the beginning of the Old Testament, were the books of Genesis, Exodus, Leviticus, and a couple of others. Then there was Samuel. He found 1 Samuel 22, and then verse 23:

"Abide thou with me, fear not: for he that seeketh my life seeketh thy life: but with me thou shalt be in safeguard."

Yes, Mr. Carlucci, you got it right. Of course you did.

Carlucci had said it was about friendship. Randy got that. It could also be about cops. How about friendship between cops?

Randy vowed then and there that he would go straight to Mack Gardner when he got back to Kansas City. First, he'd suggest they try to line up some Royals tickets for Sunday. They were playing a doubleheader against the Yankees.

Then he'd confess to lying. He had never discussed anything about publicity with Birdie Carlucci. He had not given him his word about preventing it from happening. That was a lie. But he would plead for Mack's forgiveness and then for his cooperation in keeping the Carlucci story out of the papers anyhow. He would argue that it be done for personal reasons. Even though it had only been ten weeks, he had developed a fondness for the old man, not a friendship really but a good feeling. Like it said in that Samuel verse, a desire to keep him safe, if nothing else.

"These are electric shock machines," said Harry Leonard, who had been standing by while Randy did his reading of Samuel.

Harry was pointing at two instruments that resembled small table-model radios with cords coming out of each end. Those, obviously, were stuck against the patient's temples. Randy blanched at the thought, as he did at the sight of the small waist-high stainless-steel table next to them.

"Autopsy table," said Harry, confirming what Randy had surmised. "They used them mostly to cut out brains for study. That was a big thing to do for a while."

Randy said, "I'm really impressed with all you know about the old asylum and its history."

"I told you about my father. My grandfather and grandmother—as well as an uncle and two aunts and a cousin—all worked out here too. We were a Somerset Hospital family. I grew up with the place and the people and the stories."

So Harry Leonard was from a Somerset insane asylum family the way Randy Benton was from a Missouri Pacific railroad family.

Harry, without being asked, added, "I was at Warrensburg State, aiming to become a history teacher. I had some grade problems, Vietnam came along, I didn't want to go to war, so I came back home and went to work here. They gave draft deferments then for working in state mental hospitals. I've been here ever since."

Randy's own life was slightly similar. He was in his third year in business school at U.M.–Kansas City, planning to pursue a management career with Southwestern Bell Telephone. A recruiter from the Kansas City Police Department came to campus and Randy, the son of a railroad detective, dropped by to chat. He ended up taking—and acing—the police exams, realized that being a cop was his natural destiny, became a KCPD officer upon graduation from college—and he'd been *there* ever since. It was satisfying.

Randy went over to eight or nine dark pine rocking chairs that were lined up facing a wall. With the push of a hand, he set one of them on an up-and-back movement. *Bump . . . ta, bump . . . ta.* He had heard from Birdie what *they* were all about. There were also several heavy long-handled brooms that also matched the old man's talk about rocking and sweeping being the major things for patients to do.

Then, at the end of the row of rocking chairs, he spotted two baseball bats leaning against the wall. He picked up one of them. It was a Louisville Slugger with Ty Cobb's autograph etched on it. Randy knew the name. Cobb, known as the Georgia Peach, was a great outfielder for the Detroit Tigers in the twenties and thirties.

"At least they let the patients play some baseball," Randy said, swinging the bat at an imaginary pitch. He had been a pretty fair third baseman and right-handed hitter in high school. But why was that padding—it looked like a piece of a quilt—tied around the fat part of the bat? "I never heard of anybody playing baseball with a padded bat like that, though," he said to Harry. He took another easy swing.

"I think they hit on patients with them," Harry said.

Randy said nothing. He was thinking of Josh and Birdie and wondering if either of them had ever been hit by a ball bat. . . .

"I'm really sorry we couldn't find any trace of your friend Carlucci," Harry said. "The only Carlucci I ever heard of was the company in Italy years ago that made mustard and other spicy things. I haven't seen any of their products around since I was a kid."

Randy tightened the grip on the Ty Cobb bat. "Spicy things?"

"Yeah, my mom used their tomato sauce when she made spaghetti and meatballs. I think they made oregano, powdered peppers, cinnamon, and a lot of other things too—mostly for cafés and restaurants. I think Mom got hers from a waitress friend who worked in Kansas City."

That old man just picked the name Carlucci off some old mustard jar!

Randy laughed out loud.

He raised the bat high over his right shoulder and then swung it down and around with enough force to have hit any ball thrown by anybody out of the park.

XXIII

BIRDIE

UNION STATION

1933

Josh had been gone toward Track 3 less than a minute when Birdie caught sight of a woman who looked a lot like Janice the Harvey Girl. She was coming out the employees' door by Gate 1, just a few yards from where he was standing.

It was Janice! But she was wearing a regular blue cotton dress and white sandals, her brown hair flowing down onto both shoulders. The Harvey Girl uniform, look, and starch were gone.

And she was looking right at him, walking right at him. I knew she loved me, he thought. Too bad Josh didn't see her.

Without a word of greeting, Janice said, "Two hours ago three men came into the lunchroom looking for you and your friend—not the one in the tie but the other. They described the two of you pretty well. They said there was reason to think you had come here this morning on The Flying Crow. I think they were policemen, but I couldn't tell for sure and they didn't say. I don't know why, but I told them I hadn't seen you. That could get me put in jail with you, if that's where you're headed. Is it?"

"I'd love to be in jail with you, Janice," Birdie purred.

She ignored what he said and, in her body language, was pretty much ignoring him too. "That's all I have to say to you, and I would appreciate your never telling anybody, particularly anybody at Fred Harvey's or the police, that I told you this."

And she walked away from him.

Birdie wanted to run after her.

But instead he moved off quickly in the opposite direction. He opened the employees' door, went down the stairs to the large store-room, went to the corner, opened the mirror and the other door, and disappeared inside the condiments and spices room.

XXIV

RANDY

UNION STATION

1997

On the drive back to Kansas City, Randy remembered something from that day at the Kenwood residence, something the old man had said about his life at Union Station.

It led to Randy's going to Union Station the following afternoon.

One of the restoration contractor's men found the door in the back of the old Harvey House section on the east side of Union Station and unlocked it for him. He said the door opened to a stairway that would take him up and across to the south side where Randy wanted to go.

The guy, whose first name was Roy, had worked in the maintenance department of the old Kansas City Terminal Railway Company for around thirty years. The project managers had summoned him and his memory out of retirement to help them get started. They needed Roy to tell them where all the old switches, pipes, wires, systems, nooks, and crannies were.

"There are only a few lights up there that work—that have bulbs in 'em," said Roy, handing Randy a large high-watt flashlight. Roy was a husky man with a full head of gray hair. Randy figured his age at about seventy. "But those lights and some junk and maybe some rats and a big mess is all you're going to find."

Randy had already declined Roy's offer to escort him. He wanted to do this alone.

The stairway was narrow and poorly lit. There was a strong smell of dust and grease and mold. Years as a cop had made Randy mostly immune to entering eerie or dangerous places, and he needed that conditioning right now. An ordinary person might have found this spooky and a bit daunting. There was no real sign of anybody's having been on these stairs in years, but then Randy remembered the prerestoration sweep ten weeks ago, the event that started all of this for him. Somebody must have checked this out then.

Randy put his left hand on a wooden banister and immediately jerked it back. It was caked with filth, dirt, crud. So he walked in the center of the stairway, doing his best to touch neither the banister on his left nor the flaking green wall on his right.

In a few moments, he was at the stairwell for Floor Two. Then he was at Three, after only one short zig and zag. And Four and Five. There was enough light so he had not yet had to turn on the flashlight or use it to fight off rats or any other creatures. He recalled what Birdie had said about the animals getting into the station. But there *had* been that sweep. Surely that would have flushed out anything live. . . .

FLOOR 6.

The wooden door with that number painted on it was dark, dirty, and cracked. It opened with a slight push.

It was pitch dark inside. Randy switched on the flashlight and found a light switch on the wall. A flicker of yellow light appeared from the ceiling. A lone bulb was hanging from a cord.

Roy had called it right. It was a mess of broken office furniture and stacks of rags and paper. Trash. The room itself was not that big: twelve feet square at most. The walls, like those on the stairway, were plaster, coated in a green paint that was falling off.

There was a large opening at the far side of the room.

Randy stepped over some paper bags stuffed with things he could not even imagine. Old rags, tickets, food wrappings, clothes? Who knew?

He was in the opening. Even without a light, which he could not find immediately, Randy knew what this room must have been: the dormitory. It was three times the size of the outer room. Again, with a dim light hanging from the ceiling and his flashlight he saw five, six, seven old metal cots stacked one on top of the other. Next to them were what remained of several blue-striped canvas mattresses that had clearly been feasted on by animals of some kind. There were large tears and bites in the fabric, tufts of white cotton protruding.

Randy didn't even try to imagine Birdie going at it with Janice or some woman traveler on one of those beds—if he ever really did that. If any of what he said was true. . . .

Birdie. Was that his real nickname? Birdie Carlucci, as in the name of an Italian mustard. Where was the hallway, where he said he had put the record of his life at Union Station?

Randy saw an opening at the other side of the room and walked—almost ran—toward it. It led into another small office, similar to the first one but full of metal filing cabinets and desks and chairs in various stages of wear and tear.

At the other end of it he saw a huge entranceway going off to the right. He moved to it. It was a hallway. *The* hallway? He found the light switch.

Nothing happened. The one place where he really needed light and it wasn't working. No bulb, no electricity? *Damn!*

Thank God for Roy's flashlight.

Moving its beam slowly from side to side, up and down, Randy saw that the hallway was long, maybe thirty feet to the end. It was at least ten feet wide. The ceiling was low, as in the other rooms, not more than twelve feet high.

The walls were that same green painted plaster. Some of the paint was flaked or missing. But . . . but! There were various initials, names, slogans, and dates scratched and cut into the paint. It was covered with graffiti, but a most special kind of graffiti. It looked like the train crews who slept up here decided to turn this hallway into an informal record of their presence.

There was *JCL-ATSF.* Somebody who worked for the Santa Fe? Yes. Underneath was *5/19/34.* He scratched that into this wall on May 19, 1934? Right. *Jack O.—UP—Dec 17 37.* A Union Pacific man. The initials and the names and the railroads and the dates covered every inch on both sides of the hallway. There were several scratched *MoPac* for Randy's family railroad, the Missouri Pacific. The Katy (*MKT*), the Burlington (*CB&Q*), and the others. There were dates all the way through the forties and fifties into the sixties.

Birdie, Birdie, are you really here? Where are you?

After several agonizing minutes of searching, Randy saw something that might be it. Two-thirds of the way down the hall on the right side, up near the ceiling, he saw a word that looked like *Birdie.* But the light wasn't bright enough for Randy to see it clearly from so far down.

He ran back into the first room, grabbed an old wooden office chair, and rolled it to the spot.

After determining that it would hold his weight, Randy carefully stepped up and zeroed the beam of the flashlight on the wall just below the ceiling.

BIRDIE. It had been cut into the paint in clear block letters. No question about it. B–I–R–D–I–E. There was a space and then another letter. It looked like it was an s. Yes. BIRDIE S. s for what? What was his last name: Smith? Stroud? Speakes? It could be anything. Sanders? Samuel? Hey, maybe that's it. Birdie Samuel, as in the Bible.

But that wasn't all.

Below BIRDIE S. were some dates.

11-12-35	11-12-60	11-12-85
11-12-40	11-12-65	11-12-90
11-12-45	11-12-70	
11-12-50	11-12-75	
11-12-55	11-12-80	

Why November 12? Randy, his mind whipping back to that day with the old man at the Kenwood residence, remembered Birdie talking about his birthday and how difficult it was to celebrate it alone. Didn't he say it was in November? Right. Maybe . . . probably . . .

Definitely.

Starting in 1935, two years after his arrival, he came up here on his birthday every five years and scratched the date on this wall under his name. That was the record of his life.

But he didn't make it up in 1995, two years ago. He most likely didn't have the strength to climb the stairs anymore. Or were the doors locked by then? Who knows why he didn't make it that one last time.

Randy reached into his suit-coat pocket. He held one of his car keys up and, underneath 11-12-90, he scratched 11-12-95.

That's what friends do.

NOTES AND ACKNOWLEDGMENTS

The first person to assist me in a major way was Dr. Tom Lawson, the superintendent of schools in Eureka, Kansas. He gave me a copy of his Ph.D. dissertation on the state mental hospital in Osawatomie, Kansas, that he wrote while a graduate student at Kansas State University in Manhattan. Later, in person, he also shared his thoughts and cleared the way for me to visit the present-day facility at Osawatomie.

Then came Robert Unger and Jeffrey Spivak.

Bob Unger is a former national and foreign correspondent for the *Kansas City Star* and the *Chicago Tribune,* and is now professor of journalism at the University of Missouri–Kansas City. Most important for me, he wrote *The Union Station Massacre: The Original Sin of J. Edgar Hoover's FBI,* the definitive work on the massacre. Published in 1997, it is the version of what happened on that June morning in 1933 that I went with. Bob met with me in Kansas City and allowed me to rustle through his massacre files—and his mind.

Jeff Spivak is a reporter for the *Kansas City Star* and author of *Union Station-Kansas City,* a beautifully written and illustrated book about the origin, good times/bad times, and resurrection of the station. Among other things, Jeff came with me on a tour of the building's many nooks and crannies that he arranged for me.

Another *Star* reporter, Finn Bullers, also helped me. So did Randy Proctor, Wes Cole, Kenny Servos, Doris Wesley, Fred Wiseman, Loyd Dillinger, Annette Miller, and Dr. Barbara P. Jones. I had additional assistance from the Western Historical Manuscript Collection in St. Louis and the Kansas State Historical Society in Topeka.

The last major assist—push, really—came from my editor, Bob Loomis. This book sorely needed his special brand of attention, wisdom, and hard work.

An important note on Josh's Centralia massacre recitation. His fictional recitation is based on the actual event as recounted in those five real books Will Mitchell saw on the asylum library table. *Quantrill's War* by Duane Schultz, *They Called Him Bloody Bill* by Donald R. Hale, and *Bloody Bill Anderson* by Albert Castel and Thomas Goodrich were actually published long after it would have been possible for Josh to read and memorize words from them. I exercised poet's license to include them because the books were terrific and Josh's story needed what was in them.

There were many other books that I read in the course of my research, including *John Brown's Body* by Stephen Vincent Benét, which I quoted directly. Among the others: *The Pendergast Machine* by Lyle W. Dorsett, *Institutional Care of Mental Patients in the United States* by Dr. John Maurice Grimes, *Sleep Disorders Sourcebook* edited by Jenifer Swanson, *Kansas City Southern Lines—Route of the Southern Belle* by Terry Lynch and W. C. Caileff, Jr., *Pretty Boy* by Michael Wallis, and *Reform at Osawatomie State Hospital—Treatment of the Mentally Ill 1866–1970* by Lowell Gish.

A point on the treatment of the patients at my fictional insane asylum: None of that was based on factual information about anything that happened at a Missouri institution. While derived from some general research, plus initial study involving the Osawatomie hospital in Kansas, the stories are complete fiction. As far as I know, for instance, no attendant at a Missouri *or* Kansas state hospital ever hit a patient in the head with a baseball bat. Some would argue that much worse things were done, but that's somebody else's story.

Finally, on the Union Station: Restored both inside and out to its original glory, the building was reopened on November 10, 1999. Inside, there are shops, restaurants, a movie theater, and a science museum, as well as a small space on the mezzanine that uses memorabilia to tell the story of the station itself.

But to me, there's much more there. I believe a caring, imaginative person can hear, smell, and feel the trains and the people who once made it a vibrant place of travel and adventure—and massacre. Some visitors, I suspect, might even come to understand why Birdie could make it his home for sixty-three years.

ABOUT THE AUTHOR

This is JIM LEHRER's fourteenth novel. He is the executive editor/anchor of *The NewsHour with Jim Lehrer* on PBS and lives in Washington, D.C. He and his novelist wife, Kate, have three daughters.

ABOUT THE TYPE

This book was set in Bembo, a typeface based on an old-style Roman face that was used for Cardinal Bembo's tract *De Aetna* in 1495. Bembo was cut by Francisco Griffo in the early sixteenth century. The Lanston Monotype Machine Company of Philadelphia brought the well-proportioned letter forms of Bembo to the United States in the 1930s.